Joey Phillips

Berkley's Bastards Book 2

KATHI S. BARTON

This is a work of fiction. Names, characters, places, and incidents are products of the author's imagination or are used fictitiously and are not to be construed as real. Any resemblance to actual events, locations, organizations, or persons, living or dead, is entirely coincidental.

World Castle Publishing, LLC
Pensacola, Florida
Copyright © Kathi S. Barton 2022
Paperback ISBN: 9781956788761
eBook ISBN: 9781956788778
First Edition World Castle Publishing, LLC, March 28, 2022
http://www.worldcastlepublishing.com

Cover: Karen Fuller
Editor: Maxine Bringenberg

Prologue

Yasmine started to sit up, but the pain behind her eyes had her crying out. Stopping all movement other than to lie back on the pillow, she wondered not just where she was but what had happened to get her there.

The squeak of shoes told her she was in some sort of medical facility. She'd been in enough of those over her life that even the smell of antiseptic would make her blood run cold. Not that anyone at any facility had ever been mean to her. It was just being there over and over that had her cringe whenever she smelled certain smells.

"Yasmine Dennis?" Turning her head toward the voice, she said that was her name. "My name is

Doctor Jerome. Do you know where you are?"

"Medical facility." He asked her which one. "I don't know. Has anyone notified my sister? Jasmine Dennis?"

"We've called her, but she's not arrived just yet. What can you tell me about what had you coming in here tonight?" Yasmine didn't know, but she had a feeling that not only did this man know, but he wasn't terribly happy about the turn of events that brought her here. "The police are here, Miss Dennis. They have a few questions for you about why you're here."

"All right. But I'd like to wait on my sister, please?" Dr. Jerome told her they were only going to be a moment. "I'd rather you didn't bring them in. I want to wait on my sister. You said you called her, but she's not here. I want to wait on her."

"Miss Dennis? My name is Captain Sawyer. I'd like to ask you a few questions if you'd not mind." She told him she did mind, and she wanted her sister there. "Miss Dennis, you're not in trouble. We're just here to ask you some things about last night. Do you own a car, Miss Dennis?"

"No. I will keep telling you until she's here that

I want to wait on my sister. It's important that she be here with me." He asked her two more questions, each of them sounding a little harsher, like he was angry with her now. "I would like my sister, Jasmine Dennis, here before I answer any questions you put before me."

After about the fifth time she repeated her statement, they seemed to get the idea. They weren't happy about it, but they no longer peppered her with questions.

Hearing the door open, she knew it was going to be her sister.

"Yazzie?" Thank goodness. "My goodness, what's happened to you? Why are the police here? Tell me what's going on."

"I don't know. I woke up in here, and they're asking me questions." Her sister asked someone what was going on. "Jasmine, just don't get arrested."

"We're just asking questions, for now, Miss Dennis. Some witnesses put your sister behind the wheel of a car that was the getaway vehicle for an armed robbery yesterday afternoon. There are seven dead plus three officers. We'd like to know where she was and who she was with."

"You're joking right now, aren't you?" Jasmine's fingers tightened around hers before her sister continued. "Well, I guess I can see where you'd not know. Gentlemen, I can tell you right now that there isn't any way the witness was telling you the truth. My sister has been blind since we were seven years old. There isn't any way she'd drive anything anywhere."

Jasmine made it sound like she'd won a marathon or something. That she'd come in first, too. Being blind wasn't anything Yasmine had wanted, but it had happened, and here she was. While the police asked questions of her sister, Yasmine tried to focus on anything but the fact that she was a little excited that someone, even for a brief time, thought she could be a regular person and drive a car.

"They're gone." Jasmine climbed into the bed with her and held her hands. "Your face is pretty beat up. There are bandages on your eyes. I told you to get one of those bracelet things that will tell people you're blind. What would you have done had I not come in here and saved your ass?"

"Gone to jail." Jasmine told her to be sensible. "I would have gotten around to it sooner or later,

Jasmine. It's not like I would have been able to hide the fact that I can't see from them once they asked me to look at pictures or something. Just let me lie here in the quiet for a moment."

It had only been lately that Yasmine was getting annoyed with her twin. She was forever bossing her around about this or that. Usually, things that Yasmine didn't want to do, or for that matter, didn't think necessary. Like the shirt.

Jasmine had gotten her a new shirt. She brought it to her apartment and had her try it on. She wore it for most of the first afternoon. It wasn't until she was brought back to her place after being at the mall with her that Hal, her landlord, had told her what the shirt said. "I'm blind, so pardon me for stumbling around."

The thing was, Jasmine wouldn't have seen it as a joke. Getting her a shirt that pointed out her blindness and made a big deal out of it was something that Jasmine was really good about doing. No matter how much it embarrassed Yasmine, her sister thought the world should be aware that her twin was handicapped. A word that Jasmine loved as much as Yasmine hated.

"You'll come and stay with me for a few days." Yasmine didn't bother telling her no. She wouldn't be bullied into anything at this point in her life. "That way, I can pamper you and care for you."

"I don't need caring for, Jazzie. I'm fine." She told her that she'd been beaten. "Perhaps, but it's not like I can see any more than I did before the bandages were put on my face. I'm not going home with you. I don't like your menagerie of animals. Nor do I care for all the noises at your place. The sounds or the smells."

"My home does not smell. And you'll stay with me, and that's final." Though it wasn't nearly final, Yasmine didn't say anything to her. "What is this world coming to when people are killed in a bank robbery?"

"You sound like you're rooting for the bank robbers." Yasmine was feeling sleepy and asked Jasmine to move off the bed. Of course, she had to put up a fuss. "Jasmine, blind or not, I was hurt. Just let me rest."

Calling for the nurse, her sister was just pissed off enough that she wouldn't speak to either of them. It wasn't like anyone looking at the two of them would think they were anything but related. The nurse winked at her when Jasmine didn't answer her question about the two of them being related. The only difference between the two of them that Yasmine was aware of was that her sister was annoying, and she wasn't. Laughing a little to herself, the door opened and closed before she felt the medicine kick in.

"Do you need anything else, honey?" Yasmine asked the nurse, who she assumed was giving her the medicine, where her sister had gone. "I think she's in a huff, that one. Upset because you called me in here, I guess. If you're hurting, honey, don't hesitate to call. Did they tell you how you're injured? Someone should have guessed that you couldn't see. Let me go get your chart and tell you." The door opened briefly then closed up. "Let me see here."

"You knew I was blind." The nurse, Anna, told her she had been in the room when she'd awakened. "I don't understand. I mean, I'm glad you figured it out, but how?"

"You didn't look around." She laughed a little. "It says here that you have a concussion, as well as a sprained ankle. There are fifteen stitches in your forehead, as well as numerous lacerations to your face and neck. Nothing is broken. Is there anything else I can help you with, honey?"

"No." She thought about it. "Yes. Wait. I know this is going to sound very odd, but I was wondering if you could call a friend of mine. I know his number. His name is Caleb Anderson. But I don't want you to tell my sister. She'll get all up in my face about calling someone else to help me out."

"I can do that for you." The phone was picked up, and she heard the buttons pressed. "If you don't mind my saying so, child, I think you should try and distance yourself from your sister for a bit. She's trying very hard to control you. Yes. My name is Anna Dereck. I'm a nurse at Mercy Hospital. I have a patient of mine that would like to speak with Mr. Caleb Anderson."

Control her? Yes, she supposed it would look like Jasmine was trying to control her when all she was doing was trying to keep her safe. Sometimes she did take things too far, and there were times, like now, that she wanted to get away from her. But controlling her?

The phone was put into her hand, and she said

her name.

"Hello, Yasmine Dennis. My name is Tabby Anderson. I'm Caleb's wife. He's not here right now, but I can get a message to him if you'd like." Yasmine told the other woman it was all right. It wasn't important. "I think it is. You're obviously in a hospital. Emergency room? No. It's too quiet there. What is it I can tell Caleb so he can fix whatever is wrong?"

"It's nothing, Mrs. Anderson." She said her name was Tabby. "Yes, I understand. We're friends, Caleb and me. Or we were sort of friends. I'm not sure we still are. It's been a long time, so he might not remember me at all. Well, I don't know how many blind women he knows, but I'm sure that would be the only stand out that would jar his memory."

"Are you finished ranting?" Yasmine told her she didn't feel she was ranting. "All right. Then are you finished over explaining why you'd be calling a married man? I'm assuming that's why you're rambling. I guess that would be a better word for it."

"I've been hurt, you see. I'm in the hospital with a concussion. A sprained ankle too, but since I've not gotten up, I don't know if it hurts or not.

The nurse who called for me just gave me some medication for pain, so that might be it." She felt secure in talking to this woman because she knew the chances of meeting her were slim to none. "My sister, my twin, is driving me crazy. She's...well, I was just told she's controlling. I didn't realize that before. Or maybe I did, and that was why I called you. Or Caleb. Understand?"

"I do. And even though you know you're hurt and could use someone to help you along, you don't want it to be her. Is that right?" Yasmine said that was it precisely. "You're at Mercy, the nurse said."

"Yes. But please don't bother Caleb. I was just having a moment, and now that I'm over it, I'm all right to go home with Jasmine." Before she could stop herself, Yasmine spoke again. "She has four cats and two dogs. Last time I was at her house, she had a ferret and a bird. It's very noisy at her house too. Like animals baying at the moon kind of noises." The laughter alerted her that she'd spoken aloud. "I'm sorry. You must think I'm an ungrateful sister that needs to be slapped."

"I don't, actually. I find you totally honest and fun." The door opened and closed, and she knew it was her sister by her smell. "I guess you have company now. I'll see you later, Yasmine."

"Who was that?" She told her it was a friend of hers from college. "A better friend than I am a sister? Never mind. Don't answer that. I'm sorry I got in a huff about you staying with me. But I do think it's the only way to go. You'll come and stay with me, and we'll have some fun for a while. I'll get on your nerves, and you'll go home, and we'll have a few days to reflect on how much we annoy each other before we're calling again. All right?"

Yasmine was saved from answering when her phone rang. Of course, her sister answered it and didn't even bother handing the phone to her, but just started talking to the person on the other end.

"She's asleep." Whoever it was laughed, and Yasmine had a feeling it was Tabby Anderson. "When I tell you she's asleep, then she's asleep. Who is this?"

"Give me the phone, Jasmine. I want to talk to her." Of course, she didn't. Nor did she stop telling the woman she was asleep when she had to be able to hear her talking to her sister. Then the phone slammed down on the cradle. "Why did you do that?

I told you I wanted to talk to her. Jasmine, that was just rude."

"That woman was rude. She said to tell you she had your ass. What the hell is that supposed to mean? Then she laughed at me. Like it was some kind of joke that I was trying to let you rest, as you told me you wanted to do." She did want her to let her rest, but as usual, Jasmine wouldn't do what she wanted. However, it wasn't worth fighting with her about what she wanted. "I'm going to talk to the staff and tell them you're not to have any visitors. It would be just like that rude woman to come here and try to take you from me."

"I'm not a child, Jasmine. There isn't any way she's going to kidnap me." Jasmine told her it wouldn't happen while she was there. "You're being ridiculous. Next time she calls, you hand me the phone."

"I will not. It's settled. I don't know how you think you're going to get along at home without someone there to take care of you, Yasmine. I told you it was settled, and it is. I'm responsible for you, and I take that very seriously." Jasmine had said that to her before. A lot. "Now, tell me what she said and who her name is so I can take care of this for you."

"Linda Ashcraft. She and I went to school together." Jasmine left her then, the door opening and closing told her that. Plus, she could no longer smell the cats on her sister's clothing. Yasmine smiled. "She's not going to be bothered by not coming to see me because she died some time ago. Good luck, Tabby, if you're coming here. It's going to be a nightmare for us both, I think."

Chapter 1

"Please stop." Yazzie turned toward the voice that had yelled at her. She was just angry enough to beat the person with her cane when he spoke to her closer. "There is a car right in front of you. I wouldn't have said anything, but I was afraid, with how pissed off you seem to be, that you'd knock into the car and then beat it into the ground. Just lift your cane a little higher, and you'll feel it."

"Am I still on the sidewalk?" He told her she was, but the car was illegally parked. "Okay. Sometimes I can't tell. These sidewalks are nice and even. However, unlike— I'm sorry."

"Why are you sorry?" She touched her cane to the object in front of her. Just as the man had said, there was something there that she'd have hurt herself on. "If you'd not mind, I'd like to move you out of the way of danger. Not that I don't believe you can take care of yourself, but there are people coming out of the bank that are more than likely going to be angrier than you are at the moment. And they're not going to be any happier when they figure out the police are waiting on them because of their parking."

The man didn't grab her like Jazzie would have. He only put his hand on her elbow and gently guided her off the sidewalk. There was no kind of censure in his voice either, like he was pissed because he had to help a stupid blind woman get the hell out of his way. Nor did he make fun of her. She'd only just had it pointed out to her that Jazzie did make fun of her — to other people — all the time. Instead, he told her his name.

"I'm Yasmine Dennis. Everyone calls me Yazzie. It's nice to meet you, Joey." He told her that his car was behind her if she wanted to lean against it. She did so, letting the stress of the conversation she'd just had with Jazzie a little while ago roll off her. Lifting her face to the sun she could feel beating down on her, Yazzie spoke to the man. "I'm staying with a friend of mine, Caleb Anderson. Do you know him and his wife, Tabby?"

The laughter, just a short burst of it, had her thinking he was making fun of her. Embarrassed for the second time that day, she was ready to do battle with him. People did that when they heard she was friends with a very wealthy man. Standing up, she was ready to take her chances with the men coming out of the bank and leaving when Joey spoke again.

"You're very angry all the time, aren't you? Yes, I know Caleb. He's my half-brother. And Tabby is a wonderful woman. I'm betting by now you've included her in your circle of friends." She asked him what he meant by calling her angry. "I don't know you at all, Yazzie. But you seem ready to fly off the handle every time I speak to you. You were upset when I tried to save you from hitting the car. Then again, when I laughed because you knew Caleb. I'm assuming you're always pissy. Or, and I'm thinking this is more than likely closer to the truth, someone else has pissed you off, and you're taking it out on anyone around you."

"My sister." He didn't say anything, but Yazzie felt her eyes fill with tears. "Her name is Jazzie. She's controlling me. Or trying to. I didn't realize she was doing that all along until...well, Tabby told me that Jazzie isn't a nice person for treating me like a cripple. Not in those words, mind you, but pretty close." He asked her if she thought she needed someone to control her. "I'm not sure what you mean. If you're asking me if I like her controlling me, then I'd say that's a big fat no. She was starting to get on my —"

"Hold that thought. The men are coming out, and I can tell from here that they are indeed angry. I'm going to stand in front of you, Yazzie, to make sure you're not hurt. Just stay here so that nothing happens to you." She told him she wouldn't move. "Good girl. And you're not a cripple, Yazzie. Not unless you want to be."

She could hear the men bitching. The loan they'd wanted had been turned down. Something about some land that was already sold to someone else, and they wanted more money to buy it from Anderson. Yazzie had to smile. She knew that Caleb had been buying up land all over the place.

"Mr. James? Mr. Yates? You're parked in a no parking zone. Not to mention, you're parked in a crosswalk. I'm not sure what they do where you're from, but it's against the law to park your car in a crosswalk around here." She knew the voice of the person talking. It was Billy Kimble's father, the police officer, Sher Kimble. Billy had been helping around the properties where gardens were, cemeteries and large lawns. "I'm afraid I'm going to have to write you a ticket and, since you're from out of state, you'll have to pay it today. There is no reason whatsoever for you to be—"

Yazzie didn't know the voice that interrupted Mr. Kimble. However, she figured it was one of the men who had come out of the bank.

"Are you fucking kidding me right now? What sort of petty assed town are you running around here?" Yazzie heard Joey cursing under his breath, and she had to smile. It was very colorful cursing too. "We were in a hurry, and that was the only space that was available. Suck it up, numb nuts. We're not paying any ticket. Now get the fuck out of my way before I have to move you."

"You can try that if you want. However, I'd rethink that if I were you. I'm an officer of the law, and I will arrest you if you so much as touch me." The speaker laughed. "Now, as I was saying before you rudely interrupted me. There is no reason whatsoever for you to be parking like this. There are plenty of parking spaces behind the bank had you only looked."

The sounds of something hitting the ground and a gun being fired had her reaching out to Joey. Just putting her hand on his back made her feel safe. When he told her that he had her, she believed it. It was stupid, she knew, but her eyes filled with tears again that a stranger was nicer to her than her own blood was.

"All right, Yazzie, it's all clear now." She thanked him and started for the sidewalk again. "Aren't you going to tell me the rest of the story?"

"No, that's all right. I was just complaining. I'm sorry about that. I think you have more than enough on your plate rather than being around me. You saved me today, and for that, I'm grateful." He asked her what she was going to do now. "Now? Nothing. I mean, I was just venting. You just happened to catch me when I was at a very low point. Thank you."

"Don't do that." She asked him what he meant. "Don't blow me off. I don't know why you're doing that, but please don't. I want to talk to you. About your sister. Why she made you so angry. How you met Caleb. I'm sure it's a great story."

She hesitated. To be able to vent to someone sounded really good. But just then, she decided she wanted a friend more than she did someone she could complain to. Lord knows she'd been beating herself up for so long over things that she was figuring it was about time she started letting it go. Yazzie didn't know how to vent with Tabby, who, in her opinion, knew how to say what she wanted.

When Joey told her that he was going to touch her, she felt his hand at her back as he gently moved her along the sidewalk.

"I was just about to have some lunch. I'm to understand that there are the greatest meatball subs in this place. Caleb, who I love, by the way, told me he gets them for him and Tabby all the time. I'm surprised you haven't had one with you staying there with him." She told him she wasn't allowed to have messy food in public. "While I don't know what that means, I have a feeling your sister needs to have her butt smacked. Come on, we'll have a nice and very messy lunch together."

They were handed menus, and she simply put

hers on the table. When Joey asked if there was a menu in braille, she started to protest when he put his hand over hers and handed her the menu when it arrived. Yazzie's hands were shaking so badly she wasn't sure she could make out a single word on it.

"You're going to be just fine, honey." She nodded. "You're agreeing because I think you've been taught to do so. But you really are going to be fine. Just read over the menu—" He laughed. "There are pictures on this menu. I guess I had no idea that— never mind. Just read over the menu, and we'll order our lunch. Tell me what you like to drink."

"Tea, please. Unsweet, no lemon." Putting her hands on her lap, she tried to calm her pounding heart. "I have a degenerative eye disease that has robbed me of my sight. I was about ten when it was completely gone. At first, I hid myself away from everyone, including my family. Jazzie was the only person that I would allow around me. I was a kid. Not a great excuse, but that's the truth. Then I was angry at the world. Angry at people around me that thought they had to explain everything to me as if I'd never seen green grass or the blue of the sky." She felt herself getting angry and apologized.

"You don't need to apologize to me, Yasmine. I hope you don't mind, but I do like your full name better than the shortened version. However, if you call me Joseph? Well, I guess I'd not mind if it was only you." She laughed as he had earlier, a short burst of it that had her putting her hand over her mouth. "I'm sorry you had to go through all that. And I'm sorry about your sister as well. I don't have any siblings, so I didn't learn how to share my toys as a kid. Are you married?"

"No. Who would marry me?" Realizing that she had said that too loud, Yazzie felt her face heat up. "No, I'm not married. Doubtful that I ever would be either. I mean, who would want to marry a blind woman? For all I know, I could be this really ugly woman that has the messiest hair in the world. I don't wear makeup because...well, let's face it, I couldn't tell what I was doing. I know I was a cute kid, but I have no idea what I look like now. What if I were to have a child? Goodness. I could lay it down someplace and have no idea where it was."

He ordered them each a sub, both meatball. Yazzie wasn't sure she could eat it, not in public, and waited until she thought the woman taking their order had left before voicing her concerns about it.

"First of all, I'd never let you go out with messy hair or sub sauce on your face. You're beautiful. I should have started with that. Your hair is so blonde it's like sunshine. I'm glad you don't wear makeup. It allows me to see the sprinkle of freckles across your nose. Someday I'd like to see your hair down, but you have it in a neat ponytail." She asked him if he was teasing her. When he sat down beside her in the booth, she started to move away, but he pulled her to him. "Don't pull away, please. I don't know your sister, but I can tell that I already don't care for her. I'm not sure how you're feeling is totally her fault, but I'm thinking she's a good deal of it."

Crying now, she turned her face into his chest and sobbed. He was being so nice to her that she wasn't sure how to handle the emotions she was feeling. Every word Jazzie had said to her, every mean comment, she poured out to Joey while crying. It didn't even bother her that they were in a public setting, nor that people could hear and see her. Yazzie needed someone to hold her, and if this stranger was willing to do that, she'd gladly take it.

"I'm so sorry." Joey lifted her face up by

touching her chin. "I must look a fright. When I was little, and I cried, my face would be all blotchy and —"

He kissed her. It was just a small peck to her mouth, but it made her want more. So when he brushed his mouth over hers again, she wrapped her arm around his shoulders and submitted to a kiss she knew would be nothing like she'd ever had before.

~*~

Joey watched as she picked at her sub. He'd kissed her. Now she was talking to him when he spoke, but it was jumbled and half answers. He had kissed her. Even as he sat there, trying to figure out why he was suddenly hungry, not for food but to make this woman happy, he had no idea. Kissing her had done something to his mind. And his heart.

"Are you all right?" Joey said he was just fine. "You're very quiet. I am as well. I'm not sure…. Why did you kiss me? Not that I didn't enjoy it. I did, very much so. But why?"

"Because you're beautiful. You cried on my shoulder. I don't know. But I don't regret it. Do you?" She shook her head and picked up a portion of the sub he'd cut up for her. When she took a big bite and moaned, he did as well. His mouth felt dry, and he had to take a drink before he could speak again. "Tell me how you ended up around here. I don't know that you're from here, but talk to me."

"I was hurt. Tabby and Caleb are looking into it for me. There was an armed robbery. Now that I think on it, I'm not sure where that was committed either. But the police thought I had been the driver of the car." He asked her why they'd think that. "I was beaten up badly. I mean, I don't know if I still have bruises, but I have a slightly sprained ankle as well as a concussion. My head hurts some, but not like it did that first day. Anyway. Jazzie was getting on my nerves, which is something she was doing a good deal of lately. She smells, you see."

"Smells? Are you telling me it's true that all your other senses are stronger when you lose one of them?" Laughing, Yasmine told him about the menagerie her sister had at her house. And the noise. "Christ, four cats would have been too much for me—I'm allergic. But two dogs, a ferret, and a bird would be loud. I can understand the smell part. You're not saying she stinks, but that she smells like all the animals. I would imagine if you're not used to that, it would be a sensory overload for you. How did Caleb and Tabby get you here?"

"Believe it or not, they came in the middle of the night and signed me out into their care. Not that I needed that, not really, but it was all so clandestine that I enjoyed it a little too much. The staff was asked not to tell Jazzie, and I came here to get better. Instead, she calls me all the time." He asked her how she knew Caleb, changing the subject when he could see it hurt her a good deal to speak of her sister. "His mom is who I met first. My parents thought it was a good idea to send me to public school for my education. It wasn't. Not only did I fall a great deal, as no one had shown me how to be a blind person, but the teachers were horrible to me. One told me that since I was in a public school where they didn't have the provisions for someone like me, I'd have to learn however I could, without their extra help. I can understand where they were coming from. Now, anyway. But all I could see then was that I was a handicapped person in a world of seeing people. Ms. Anderson got me into a specialized school, and they not only taught me how to function among seeing people but also that my hearing was better than most. I can hear a voice and tell you, even months later, who is speaking. Perhaps not their name if no one tells me, but I can pick them out of a crowd. Not terribly useful as a skill, but I can hear a language and know it well enough to pass for a native. I might not be able to read their newspaper, but I can tell you what the conversation is about."

"That's a wonderful talent. When I was in the service, I certainly could have used someone with those skills. I can't tell you how many times we'd be given a chart of phrases and not have any idea how to pronounce them. We didn't do blending well." They both laughed, and he noticed that she'd finished more than half her sub. He didn't mention it to her, knowing he'd embarrass her again. "So is that what you do for a living? Listen to languages?"

Joey had only been joking, but when she nodded, he asked her what she did. "I sit in a room all day and listen to recordings of conversations that agencies from all over the world send me. Sometimes it's just books I'm working with someone on, like an author that might be using a translator program on their computer, and it's not right. It's a lot of fun, and it pays me very well, enough to have a nice place to stay. Speaking of which, I need to go back there soon. I can't stay with Caleb forever."

It was on the tip of his tongue to tell her she could come and live with him. But he stopped himself. When the check was laid in front of him, he looked at the bill and smiled at the note that was written there. Caleb had seen them together and had picked up their bill. Joey told Yasmine what had happened.

"He doesn't have the wrong idea about us, does he?" Joey asked her what idea she had about them. "None. I mean...no, I don't know. Is there something?"

"I hope so. I'd like to see you more. Have a dinner or a lot of dinners with you. Even if we were to only come here once a week and have a meal, I'd consider myself lucky." Her cell phone rang, and he was surprised to hear it tell her that the caller was Jazzie. "I didn't know you could get that sort of app on your phone. I might like that too when I'm working and can't get to it to just see who it is."

"It's also a pain in my butt." She didn't answer the call, and he heard it say that it was going to voice mail. "She's very angry with me. So much so that she told me she was going to call the police on me.

I haven't any idea why she'd think they'd care, but that's her threat. She told me I've betrayed her. That I should be more grateful to her for all she's had to sacrifice taking care of someone like me."

"Has she? Sacrificed her life for you?" Yasmine told him she wasn't sure who was doing the sacrificing. "I see. You sound like a person who has had the light shined on your life now and are not sure how to move forward."

"That's it exactly." She cocked her head, and he watched her as she was listening. "The man from earlier just came into the restaurant. He's looking for a *fella*, he said, by the name of Phillips. I can only assume it's you. His voice is tight with anger. I don't know where we are in relationship with the door, but can he see you?"

"No. We're in a booth at the back of the restaurant. If I asked you to stay here, would you?" She told him she was blind, not stupid. Laughing, he spoke again. "I'm going to go see what he wants. I'm armed, as it's part of my job to help the police when they need it. Also, I'm wearing a vest in the event you might be worried about my being hurt."

"I am, as a matter of fact. But you don't have

a bullet—" He was glad he was looking at her when she frowned, cocking her head again. "He's armed. The man has mentioned it to the other man he's with. I don't know the other man, as I didn't hear anyone speaking earlier, but he's told him to go outside the restaurant and make sure no one leaves. I think he means to hurt people until he finds you. Please be careful."

"I will. Can you call the police for me?" She said she would, right away. Standing up, he kissed her on the mouth. "That's for luck. Just stay here until me or Caleb comes for you. All right?"

"Yes."

He moved in and out of the tables, keeping the barrier poles between him and the men. He could see them now and knew Yasmine had been right. It was the idiots from earlier. When he was just behind the two of them, Joey asked them what they wanted with him.

The man who had been telling Sharon, the hostess, that she'd better be getting him to come here or she'd be in trouble turned to eye him. Joey wanted to back away from the anger he could see on the other man's face.

"I asked you what you want. I'm here having a nice lunch with my girlfriend, and you're messing that up. I believe you were told you can't purchase land that isn't for sale, and that should be the end of it." He told Joey he knew the owner. "So? I'm sure there are many others that own property around here who I know. It's not for sale. Shut up and move on."

"I had a deal with the banker hereabouts." Joey didn't bother telling him that not only was the banker not going to help him, but he doubted very much if anyone would after this. "I want that land sold to me. I have plans for it."

"I would say it sucks to be you then, but I'm reasonably sure it sucks to be you at any time in your life." The man pulled out the gun then, and Joey had a feeling he could get a message to Yasmine without shouting. "You just pulled a gun on me? Why? Do you think I have that kind of pull that you can hold me up for the land to be sold to you? Mr. Anderson, as I'm sure you've been told numerous times, isn't willing to part with his land. He purchased it free and clear, and there is shit you can do about it."

"So I've been told. But I know everyone has a price. I'll just offer him more than he paid for it, and we'll be building some mighty fine shopping malls out there. A few hotels too. You'll see. These dumbasses around here, they'll be worshiping at my feet, I'll bring in so many jobs. What has Anderson done for this place."

"He put my son through college for nothing." The people around the table started telling the man what Anderson had done for this town.

"Helped me figure out how to get a grant to put me one of those tin roofs on my house when it blew off a few weeks ago. He didn't call us dumbasses either."

"Last week, that beautiful wife of his came to my house and helped me with arrangements when my momma died."

Person after person got up to speak about the things Caleb had done for this town, on both a professional and personal level. Joey saw Sher outside the window where they were and nodded at him when he made a motion for him to get the man outside.

"If you wish to discuss this further, we can. You two leave here, and I'll go with you willingly. I'll even set you up a meeting, without weapons, to speak to

Mr. Anderson." He saw Caleb then and glanced in the direction of Yasmine. Tabby was guiding her out the back of the place. "I'm sure you can talk to him at great length on the things you're wanting to do with his property."

Joey's sense of relief of seeing Yasmine no longer in the building made his knees weak. Nearly missing what was being said to him, he asked dumbass to repeat himself. Then he did something he hoped the hell he'd not regret.

Snatching the gun from the man, he jerked the talker around until he was in a headlock. He heard something snap and knew he'd just killed the man. Joey was holding his gun on the other man just as Sher came into the place. His anger at having a gun pointed at him wasn't nearly as sharp as when he thought Yasmine was being threatened just by being in the restaurant.

"Hiya, Joey. Looks to me like you got your hands full there. Can I help you out some?" He told him what he thought he'd done to the man in his arms. "Self-defense. No other way is anyone going to look at it. I'll have to take you in, as you're aware, just to get some answers, but we all saw the gun he had pointed at you."

"This man is holding a gun on my forehead. Can someone please arrest him?" Sher laughed, and Joey felt better for hearing it. "This is one fucked up town if you ask me. This man attacked us and killed my cousin. I want you to arrest him. I'm pressing charges."

"You just hold your horses there a little bit while I take care of things with your— Did you say your cousin?" Sher felt for a pulse and apparently didn't find one, as he shook his head at Joey. "No hope for it, I'm afraid. He's dead. That's what happens when you pull a gun on someone smarter than you. Let him go, Joey, and I'll call the coroner to have him taken away. Then we'll take this idiot in. I'm assuming you're pressing charges?"

"Yes." The other man started saying how he'd said it first. That he wanted to press charges. "It's not a contest. However, I think mine will stick better than yours will. You did come in here with the intent to harm. Not to mention, your cousin pulled a gun on me while you just stood there. That's aiding and abetting."

When the other cops came into the restaurant,

he was relieved of his burden. Joey could see that he'd indeed broken the man's neck. His neck was at a grotesque angle, and it looked as if his head could turn around completely. It wasn't until the other man left that Sher spoke to him again.

"He didn't grieve much, did he?" Now that he'd mentioned it, the cousin hadn't said anything other than he was going to press charges against Joey. "Well, I guess it takes all kinds. Come on, buddy, let's get you outside before Yazzie has a fit. She was telling—well, telling them is a bit understated—the men out there that you're to be kept safe."

When he was out into the sunshine, he lifted his face to it. There had been a time when he never noticed things like sunshine, or even if the sun was up or not. A short breeze blowing over trees, making them sway in a sort of slow-motion dance. Since being given a second chance, like Caleb had given him, he'd been doing a lot of looking around. Smelling the roses, so to speak. When a hand touched his chest, he looked into the face of Yasmine.

"Hello, beautiful." She laughed, and he smiled. "I was wondering if you'd have dinner with me tonight since our lunch was rudely interrupted by some not so nice people."

"You called me your girlfriend. Why would you let people know that? I mean, I have pointed out that I'm blind. Unless you are too. You have to see that I can't be your girlfriend. I can be a girl that's your friend, but we both know that's about all we can be to each other." He asked her why. "Why? You must be hard of hearing. I said I'm blind. That will never go over well with anyone."

"I don't care what other people think. And yes, we can make this work because I would like for you to be my friend and girlfriend." Joey kissed her. "Now that we have that settled, how about you and I go over to the police station and fill out whatever we need to so we can get to know each other. Also, I need to find a house. I nearly forgot that Caleb set me up with a realtor to look at them."

"You're nuts." Joey thanked her. "It wasn't meant as a compliment, moron. I suppose you want me to go with you to your house hunting. If so, you have to know that I'm not going to be able to give you any kind of advice on it. I sort of have this disability that doesn't allow me to see shit. You're aware of that too, I'm assuming."

"Yes. Yes, I am."

He was still laughing at her when they got to the police station. Even here—the place wasn't all that busy, but a jail house would depress many—he felt good. When he was finished up, he called Caleb to get the realtor's name and number. Joey thought this was going to be the most fun he'd had in a while.

Chapter 2

"I've been able to get in touch with Martin Hamilton. He's going to pick up a cell phone at the store so we can talk privately. The place he's staying is a boarding house, and there is only one phone. It hangs on the wall in the kitchen where the landlady hangs out until your call is— What's happened? You seem upset." Tabby told him she was. Very much so. Caleb put his file away and asked his wife what was going on. "You have to tell me so I can slay the dragons or whatever you need done. Is this about Yazzie?"

"Mostly her sister, but yes. I was wondering if you knew someone that could do a deep-deep background check on someone. Jazmine." Caleb asked her what had happened that would make her want that. "Yesterday, Yazzie came to me and asked me if I knew how to destroy a phone. I said you only had to break it in half or something, and she said it had to be destroyed, not just broken. I suggested that I take the phone and look up how to completely destroy a cell phone. There were about fifteen messages on it. All of them hadn't been read, so I listened to one of them, just to make sure she wasn't having me destroy something and would need the messages later."

"They were from Jazzie, correct?" Nodding, Tabby pulled out the phone and sat it on the desk. "You didn't destroy it?"

"I couldn't. Not until I talked to you about it. This is the first message on the phone. I'm sure there were more of them, but this is the point where Yazzie stopped listening to them. I'm thinking her sister is going to hurt her in some way. Or at the very least, take her back to the dark place she was in at one time." He asked her what that meant. "It's here, in this message. Apparently, Yazzie tried to commit suicide once. Or more, I don't know yet. But I'm going to find out if Jazzie is the reason for her feeling that was her only solution."

Caleb waited while she set up the speakers on the phone. He didn't have any brothers or sisters when he was growing up, so he wasn't sure of the dynamics of having a sibling. As soon as the message started, he could only stare at Tabby as it played.

"'What the ever-loving fuck do you think you're doing not answering me, Yazzie? When I find you—and don't you dare think I won't—you're going to be in a world of trouble. You're my sister, and I'm responsible for you and your welfare. You have no idea how much I have sacrificed to make sure you have a roof over your head and food in your cabinets.'" Tabby pressed the pause button and explained to him that Yazzie had a well-paying job that was well into the six figures, so she didn't understand that part of the conversation. After pressing play again, he listened to the rest of the message. "'You get your ass back here, and I'll set you straight on a few things. And if you think you can do this again, I'll have you locked up so quickly again that your head will spin. And there will be no more attempts on your life, either, unless you need me to do it for you. At this point, I'd gladly help you overdose or even to slit your wrists. Come back here so I can help you, or so help me, Yazzie, I'm going to hurt you.'"

"Why does she feel that Yazzie needs to come home?" Tabby told him what was on the other messages. "So she feels like Yazzie being a cripple— does she actually call her that? Never mind, I know she does. She feels that Yazzie being a cripple makes it so that she is responsible for her wellbeing. I don't know if you've noticed this or not, but I doubt very much that Yazzie has had anyone looking after her well being for a while. In actuality, I think since she's been here, she's blossomed. Like she's becoming stronger in her voice. Also, I know that I mentioned this to you before, but Joey and her are out looking at houses today. Together."

"Do you think they'll become a couple?" Caleb said he thought the only hold up for them not to be was her. "She's had it beaten into her that she's not good enough for anyone for so long that Joey might have to show her that she's perfect for him. I love her. She's very smart and outspoken. I bet if you were to ask her, she'd be willing to do just about anything to keep away from her sister. I know I would. That's why I want to have someone look into Jazzie and see what her deal is. Another thing I'd like to know is how is she affording the nice car she has. As well as a couple of more big-ticket items, like a big boat and a large Olympic-sized pool at her home that I've seen on her social page. Jazzie goes to a lot of parties too. I'm not sure what that might have to do with her wanting her sister back home, but it's something to think about."

"There is the driving the getaway car in that robbery that Yazzie was initially questioned about." He told Tabby what he'd been able to find out about why Yazzie had been accused of being the driver of the car. "I'm still looking into who beat her up so badly and why. Also, who found her? How did she end up in the hospital? Yazzie doesn't know. She just woke up there. When I asked her what she'd been doing before, before the hospital, she told me she'd been having dinner at her sister's house. I'm getting the toxicology report sent to me later today that they took at the hospital."

"Did she drug her?" Caleb told her he didn't know, but it looked like it. "Caleb, do you suppose Jazzie was driving the car, and she needs to keep her sister under lock and key so she can continue doing that sort of thing? I'd not put anything past her at this point."

"That was my first gut feeling when she told me where she'd been. And as my mom used to tell me, go with your gut. It'll never turn you in the wrong direction."

Tabby sat there for several minutes without commenting. Caleb watched her. She was a thinker, and he loved that about her. He loved her, simply put.

"We need to figure out what she does for a living. Also, what part, if any, she played in the robbery. I'd like to see the footage the police have that would have them looking at Yazzie, of all people." He said he knew someone that might be able to help. "All right. Can you work on that then? I mean, this is some serious shit going down here. I don't want any of us hurt, but especially that girl if she's an innocent in her sister's plot to get her into trouble."

"I'll have someone looking into it today. I don't know for sure when they can get back to me, but I'm sure they'll do it." She nodded and stood up. "Tabby, what about this phone? I hate that we still have it when she thinks it was destroyed."

As if he'd said her name, the phone startled him when it rang. The picture that came up was of Jazzie. He had never met the other woman, but her name was under the picture. Now that he thought about it, he did know her. Making sure he didn't answer it, he held the phone up to Tabby.

"I know her. While we were on campus once, Yazzie was visiting my mom and came to see me, and this woman was there. It made me uncomfortable seeing her following us around like she was stalking us. I didn't mention it to Yazzie. I wish now that I had, but Mom noticed her too." Tabby asked him if she ever approached them. "No. Not at all. When I started for her once to ask her what the fuck she was doing, she ran off. I wish now that I'd paid more attention to what she was doing hanging out with us. Do you suppose she does that all the time? Follows her around like that to make sure...I don't know, make sure she can keep tabs on her?"

"I'd say that's about right. Christ, this is getting weirder and weirder all the time. Why would someone stalk their own sister? What sort of person calls their own flesh and blood a cripple? Not a few times either. Why does she have such a hard-on for her sister to come back to where she was living? I mean, it's not really that far. We drove there in less than two hours to get her." He said he didn't know, but he was going to make a couple of calls now. "Good. I'll talk to Yazzie about still having her phone. You're right in that. We don't want her to find out and be upset with me about it."

After she left, he picked up the phone to make a call. He didn't actually know the president, but his mother had, and he figured after using the personal number his mom had used to call him for Joey, he might be all right with him asking for another favor. All he could do was say no, he told himself.

Laughter greeted him when the phone was answered. "Hello, Caleb. I'm so glad you called. I have some information for Joey if he's around." He said he wasn't, but he'd have him call. "You do that. What is it I can do for you?"

After explaining what he was looking into, then requesting a little help, the noises in the background were cut off. Apparently, the man had gone into a room and closed the door.

Sitting up straighter in his chair, Caleb told him

he was sorry. "I should have just emailed you. But this is something that is bothering Tabby and myself. The woman is a little off the rails, as my mom was fond of saying, and I'd like to get to the bottom of it. Not to mention, Yazzie and Joey are seeing each other, and—well, seeing each other is a little premature, but they are getting to know—" President Davis said his name. "I babble when I get nervous."

"Your mother did as well. I surely miss that woman. She could love you to pieces and burn your butt in the next second if she thought you were slacking in any way." He heard papers shuffling then. "Joey made a call to me yesterday about the same thing. He told me that he also wanted a background check on himself in the event it came up. I don't know under what circumstances a background check would come up, especially on such a good man, but I did it. Do you have a fax machine? I know they're sort of out of date, but it's much better than an email, if you ask me, if you don't want anyone to know what you're sending."

After giving him the number, wondering if his mom had told the president that or he had told her, he watched as several sheets of paper came through the machine while he explained. He also begged him to call him Charlie and to stop calling him sir.

"I have a meeting in about ten minutes that I cannot miss. Once I'm finished up with that, I'll call you back. It might be late, around nine. No later than ten. Would that be all right?" Caleb told him t would be fine, then asked if Joey could see the paperwork as well. "Yes, of course. He did ask me for it. It was much easier for me to get him to call me Charlie than I'm having luck with you. You go over that paperwork, and we'll discuss it later."

After looking over the first couple of pages, he knew just enough about Jazmine Dennis to think that Joey was correct in asking for background checks. It wasn't until Caleb was closing up the paperwork into a file that he noticed there were satellite pictures in the middle of the sheets. Pulling one of them out, he looked right into the face of the woman who was driving, he assumed, the getaway car at the bank.

Picking up his phone again, this time his cell, he called Joey. He hated to tell him what he'd done when he was in such high spirits when he answered the phone on his end. Telling him what he'd been doing as well as talking to Charlie, he heard the laughter die as if someone had murdered it for him. Trying hard to tell him things he'd seen in some of the paperwork wasn't helping him. It wasn't until Joey spoke that he found out what was going on at his end.

"We've just about found us a house. I'm having some trouble convincing Yasmine to move in with me, but I think I'm wearing her down. There will need to be some— Caleb, I know what you're telling me without telling me, so listen up. Okay? I knew what you were going to find. I think Yasmine does as well." He told him he was sorry. "Don't be. We're having a wonderful time, and I'm not going to allow any news like this to spoil her fun. Can we do this later? I will tell her what I've done, but I want to do it someplace quiet. Not here."

"Yes, I understand. Why don't the two of you come here for dinner tonight? We'll cook out and have a good laugh or two first." He said that would be wonderful. "I'm sorry to have disturbed you. But I didn't want you to come around and find out that I have your paperwork."

"No big deal, Caleb. We're family, right? I do hope you remember that." Caleb was touched and told the other man that. "Good. I like to keep you on your toes. All right. We're about done with looking at this house. We're headed to the last one now. It has a larger back yard and more bedrooms. I haven't any idea why you thought we'd need any more than a couple of bedrooms. I know you said you'd help me with financing, but some of these are out of my price range. But we're having fun. I'll talk to you later."

After getting off the phone with Joey, he leaned back in his chair. All the houses Joey was looking at were homes he and Tabby had purchased right after getting married. It was for his family. Joey, since he was the first to arrive here, got first pick. Then as they arrived, the men would take the one they wanted. He had no idea what he'd do if the last to arrive didn't care for the last house, but he'd figure it out.

Caleb wanted to get to know his brothers. Help them in any way he could too. Of the six bastards of Howard Berkley, he was in the best position to help them in every way that they might need.

~*~

Joey loved this house. After walking around with Yasmine, pointing out the things he loved, she finally turned to him. She had the most beautiful face, and he was thinking that he was falling in love with the temperamental beauty.

"You love this house. I can almost feel it from you." He told her he did indeed love this house. "You do know that as large as I can tell it is, we could live here forever and not see each other much. Would you like that?"

"No. I want to see you a great deal. Naked too, if you'd allow it." Joey loved it when her face got all pink like it was now. "I need to tell you that I'm not teasing about that. You're making such an impression on me that I could easily spend the rest of my life with you and never grow tired of being with you. Naked or not."

"You're just horny, that's all." He burst out laughing. That was another thing he was in love with—her hold nothing back attitude when she spoke. "Have you made a decision?"

"Yes, this is my favorite house. I can see you and I spending the rest of our life here, naked or not. Also, I've decided I'm going to invest in lots of bells. That way, if we have any children, we can put bells on them, and you can use your super power to find them in this house. I'll help you, of course, but I have to admit, watching you looking for where you placed our children is going to be fun."

"You've got us growing old here in this house and having babies. That's not going to work with us avoiding each other." Joey pulled her into his arms and kissed her, much to the amusement of their realtor. "He's going to take this one, Ms. Roberts. I think he's nuts. How many bedrooms does this place have anyway?"

"Twelve."

When the realtor wandered off, telling them she'd be putting in the paperwork for this house, Joey waited until she was out of sight before he kissed Yasmine again. However, she turned her head before he could take full advantage of her sexy little mouth.

"Spill it. Whatever is bothering you, I want to know what it is before I agree to anything with you. And that means even going back to Caleb's home for dinner. I did hear you say that to him." He nodded, then told her they were going there for dinner and to talk. "You've found out something you don't think I can handle. And you're keeping it from me because why?"

"It's about your sister. I'm not sure of all of it,

but enough to know it has Caleb a little concerned. I told you I was going to have a background check done on her, right?" She said he had told her, yes. "Well, it's with Caleb. I guess he was calling in a favor to have it done as well. When he called my buddy, he told him I'd already requested it. Are you still ready to get the dirty secrets about your sister and myself?"

"I don't know why you think I'd want dirty secrets about you. I've told you a million times that we're just having fun." He didn't tell her it was well beyond having fun for him. And sometimes, when he saw her thinking, he knew it was more than that for her as well. "Joey, we're going so fast with this. I will admit that I think I love you. I don't know for sure because my mind is a whirl of thoughts every time I'm near you. Don't get me started on how fuzzy my head and heart are when you kiss me. It's so fast I'm waiting for the other shoe to drop."

"There is no shoe dropping, love. And I've fallen in love with you as well." She leaned her head on his chest, and he held her there. "Caleb is having us over for dinner tonight, so we can go over what was dug up on Jazmine. He also found some things we can look over about the robbery you were thought to have driven the car for. I'm waiting on the reports back on the blood that was drawn when you were first brought in. A friend of mine in the hospital is working on getting me a copy of the report."

"It was Jazzie, wasn't it? The person driving the car." He said it looked like it. "I don't know why, but I think I knew that even when they were accusing me of doing it. She was just too...I don't know how to say this without it coming out wrong, but she was just too happy to tell them I'm blind. And I was told a few weeks ago, by a friend of mine, that Jazzie is wearing her hair like I do mine when she's out. Pulled back in a ponytail. Jazzie hates it when I pull my hair back. She says that it makes me look more crippled than ever. You know, I fucking hate that word. I don't want to say it ever again."

"Good. I hate it as well." When Ms. Roberts returned with the paperwork, Joey said he'd talk to Caleb about the house. "He's helping me out with financing."

"The house is yours, Mr. Phillips. It was purchased about two weeks ago by Mr. Anderson, along with four other houses. He said he was bringing his family home, and he'd need to make sure they had plenty of home to live in." Joey asked her if she was sure. "Yes. I only need to ask you if you want Ms. Dennis's name on the deed too. Then I'll file it for you."

Both he and Yasmine answered her at the same time. His was to say yes, her name was on the deed too, and Yasmine was saying no. Since he knew this was the next move in their being together, he told Ms. Roberts to go ahead and put Yasmine's name on there right next to his. As soon as she had them signing off on the paperwork, Ms. Roberts left them. The keys, she told him, were on the kitchen counter.

"Do you want to have a look around our first and hopefully last home, Yasmine?" She stood in front of him with her arms over her chest and her foot tapping. "If you're thinking that's going to intimidate me, you're wrong. All I can think of is how sexy you look right now. And imagining you doing this to our children."

"I'll lose them." He laughed, pulling her to him again. But she sidestepped him and was standing near one of the windows he'd described to her earlier. "Joey, don't you get it? I might even pass this blindness to them. Then what will you do?"

"Love them as much as I do you. Blindness isn't the end all of everything, Yasmine. You being blind didn't stop me from falling in love with you. It won't our children either. However, if you don't want to have children, we can adopt if you wish. Or have both. I'll love them no matter where they come from." She told him to be serious. "I am. I'm about as serious as I've ever been in my life."

She started pacing, and he was careful not to laugh when she had to put her hand out before she turned at the end of the long room. Joey thought for sure she'd murder him in his sleep if he laughed.

"What if Jazzie is a bad guy?" He asked her why that should matter to them. "She might, I don't know, try and blame me for some of her woes. She has for everything else that has happened to her. Did I tell you she was engaged to be married once? Apparently, the man wouldn't marry her because of me being so clingy. I don't remember being clingy at any time in my life. She has been, however. Forever wanting to know every detail about my life and what I do for a living."

"She hasn't any idea what you do for a living? I don't either, but I thought we'd get to that eventually.

I know you told me a little." Yasmine told him she worked as a translator for the CIA. "No shit? That's wonderful. I bet that's a good job."

"It is. And the pay is really good too. Of course, Jazzie seems to think I have no idea how to manage my money. I guess being blind to her means I'm a cracker short of a meal or something." He laughed, and turned it into a cough when she glared in his direction. "I have been investing my money wisely. Ms. Anderson taught me that. I might have had a late start on putting my money to work for me, but I have. Since you're insisting that we live together and have babies that I'm sure will be lost in this house, I'll say that *we* have a nice nest egg."

"Oh, that's not all I want. I want you to become my wife. Forever." She stiffened, and he waited for her to tell him it wasn't what she wanted. When she moved closer to the wall, he did as well. Whispering because it seemed to be the right thing to do, he asked her what she heard. "I can call Caleb or the police if you think I should."

"Jazzie is out there." He pushed Yasmine closer to the wall and used his body as a shield while she explained to him what she heard. "Her car. It has one of those strangely loud mufflers on it. That's what I heard."

"I'm going to go and check. She hasn't any idea who I am, so I'll be able to go out on the front deck and have a look around. Will you stay here?" She nodded, but he could see the fear on her face. Looking around, he decided he didn't care for her being alone in the house if he left her. "Yasmine, I'm going to put you in the hall closet here. There is no lock on the door, but if she gets by me, at least she won't be able to see you standing out in the open. All right?"

"Yes, all right."

Joey had no idea why, but her agreeing so readily worried him a great deal. Putting her in the closet with the light on, he laughed at himself when he realized that on or off, she'd not know the difference. So he turned it off again so there would be no light under the door.

Leaving the door open just enough to allow Yasmine to hear should it be her sister, he stepped outside and could see that it was indeed Jazmine. He watched her getting out of the car that was one he'd only seen in magazines. Powerful and expensive.

Everything about Jazmine had him thinking she was used to having money and hordes of it.

"May I help you?" Jazmine smiled up at him, and he could see the resemblance between her and Yasmine. With her hair pulled back the way it was right now, he'd bet anything that it was a look she was going for. "If you're here to have a look at the house, I'm afraid it's been purchased."

"No, I'm not here for the house. But I was told my sister might be out here. Helping some guy with his house. I don't know what she could do to help him. She's a cripple." Joey wanted to tell her she wasn't but held his tongue. "Well? Have you seen her?"

"I don't know who you are, so I'm not going to tell you if I've seen someone you claim to be your sister. And even if I did see her, I'd certainly not tell someone that has the nerve to call their own flesh and blood a cripple. You do know that's not all that nice, don't you?" She waved him off as she moved closer to the house. "As I said, this house has been sold. To me. And as of right now, you're trespassing. So either get into your car and get off my land, or I'll call the cops and have them—"

"Whoa there. You sure went south fast. I thought small towns were friendlier than you all seem to be around here. I only came here to see if my *crippled* sister was out here. And yes, I know it's not nice, but she's my sister that I have to keep in line, so I'll call her whatever I want. So, have you seen a blind woman stumbling around here or not? Her name is Yasmine Dennis. Mine is Jazmine Dennis. If you've seen her, you must tell me. I have to take her home and make sure she stays put this time. There is no telling what sort of things could happen to her the way she trips over every little thing."

"Leave, Ms. Dennis, before you piss me off more." Joey was pissed, too, over the fact that she was talking about Yasmine like she was nothing more than an idiot that needed to be guided around on a leash. "You have until the count of five before I call the police. If you're still here, or even come near this house again, I will shoot you. I'm done with your ass as of right now. One."

He was to three when she finally got into her car. Knowing on some level that she was going to cause him trouble when she left, he turned his back to her car spinning out as she got down the drive. Looking up, he saw Yasmine standing there, laughing hard. It was more than he could have hoped for after dealing with her sister.

Chapter 3

Yasmine zoned out. It was that, or her head was going to explode. There was just too much. Too much information. Too much wrong. Just simply too much of everything. There wasn't even any way for her to process some of the things that had been found out.

Jazmine had two children. Well, she gave birth to them, but she didn't keep them. Caleb mentioned finding them to make sure they were in a good place, but Yasmine was beginning to feel overloaded by then. She didn't remember answering him.

Jasmine was also wealthy, even though she'd never worked a day in her life—there were no hits on her social security number for ever having used it other than for a driver's license. She had a boat. Homes all over the world. Cars that cost more than she'd ever thought a simple conveyance could cost. And through it all, Yasmine had been giving her money to care for her needs.

Going to the grocery store for her was done by a service. Jazmine would have it delivered to her door, then take it to her. Doctors' appointments were done in one of her staff's cars. Yasmine was told she'd done that so she'd not know about her other cars. There was more too. A great deal more than her mind, but mostly her heart, could deal with right now.

"Yasmine?" She told Tabby she was all right. "No, you're not. I don't know what you're thinking, but I want you to know we're all here for you. Your sister is a piece of work. I'm sure you realize what sort of things she's been doing behind your back."

"No. She's been doing these things right there in front of me. I bet she had a good laugh about it too. Being pregnant with two children while I never had a clue. Christ, I was so naive." Tabby told her she'd trusted her. "Yes, I did. And look what that got me. A sister more evil than anything I've ever encountered.

Not to mention all the money I've given her over the years. What do you suppose she did with it? I'm betting she burned it. While laughing about how her poor dumb sister didn't have one brain cell that worked."

The slap to her face was startling. Yasmine supposed it was painful as well, but to think that Tabby had hit her really had her wanting to cry. She asked her what that was for.

"You're whining. I hate whiney people." Yasmine told her she was sorry. "Don't do that either. Don't be sorry for what your sister did to you. She should be sorry. Hell, Yasmine, I think you should make her sorry that she ever fucked with you. While I don't have a plan just yet, you can bet your ass that we'll have one before too much longer. When I think of…. Well, I'm not going to go into all that again, but we are going to get her ass in jail. Then prison."

"Didn't Joey say something about the robbery?" Tabby explained what he'd said. "So she let them see her, dressed and looking like me. That way, she could throw them off the scent, so to speak. I don't know if Jazmine looks like me or not as an adult. I don't get hugs from her. I don't sit close to her when we're at my place. We did as kids—I mean, we are twins. However, her hair was dark while mine was blonde. For that matter, I have no idea what color my hair is now either. When I've gone to the salon with her to get a trim, she could have had them make me purple for all I would have known about it. And now I wouldn't put a damned thing past her."

"Your hair is a pretty blonde color. It's trimmed nicely, and you wear it in the messy, probably not on purpose, ponytail in the back. You have a few freckles across your nose that seems to match up perfectly with your light brown eyes. There is a small healing scar on your left cheek. More than likely from the beating you took, which we're still trying to figure out. You're very slim. Not thin, just slim and toned. You're tanned, but not overly so." Yasmine thanked her for that. "No worries. Also, you have in earrings. They're diamonds if I don't miss my bet. And a little off. Like you did it at home and didn't quite get them lined up right."

"I did it, believe it or not. My mother wouldn't allow me to get them done when I was a child. She said she had too many other things to worry about with me that I didn't need to add to her list. So the day after she and my dad passed away, I did it in an act of defiance." Tabby giggled with her. "I have this system for my clothing. I only wear one or two colors of pants or shorts that I can match up with any color of shirts. Thankfully I can order online by voice, and when they arrive, I'm pretty much guaranteed they'll be what I wanted."

"Smart girl. Your top is a beautiful shade of teal. Your shorts are a lighter shade of tan. Your shoes are tan too. How do you do that? Know which shoes match which outfit?" Yasmine told her. "We'll have to get you something other than tan shoes when we go out. You can bet that I'll not steer you in the wrong direction."

"I'm going to be staying with Joey in his new home." Tabby congratulated her. "I hope we can get along. I've fallen in love with the big lug. He's wearing me down on a lot of things. I'm getting more confident too. About all sorts of things."

"He's a good man. He and Caleb are getting to know each other. However, you'd not believe they are only half-brothers. They look a great deal alike. Not twins, though they are fairly close in age, but hair color. Eyes. Even their build is the same." Yasmine asked about the other men Caleb was related to. "There were seven counting Caleb. However, one of them, I think his name was Jonathon Warner, took his own life. The others have been notified by courier, but we've not heard back from any of them. Caleb is disappointed, but he said if he doesn't hear from them soon, he'll go find them."

"I love that he's doing this. His mom would have been so proud. She was an amazing woman. And she had such a good heart too." Tabby asked her when she'd met her. "I was about nine at the time. My sight was already gone by then. I was at a doctor's appointment and had been told there was nothing they could do for me. I left — well, ran away from the office sobbing about how my life was ruined. I ran into her. Literally. She picked me up and dusted me off, and asked me what was going on. Up until then, I'd been trying to make it in a regular school, you see, and it wasn't easy to be blind with kids who were about as cruel as Jazzie is. It just occurred to me. I wonder if she had anything to do with that. Anyway. The next week I was given a full scholarship to a blind school that taught kids and adults how to deal with their new issues. It was the first time I'd been helped and my first trip away from home. I stayed there all the school year and sometimes summers for extra credit. It's where I learned that I can hear things and remember them. I've never told anyone that before. Not even Jazzie."

"More than likely a good thing too. She might well have used it against you." Nodding, she thought that Tabby was correct. "Yasmine, can I ask you a personal question? You don't have to answer if you don't think it's any of my business, but why were you paying your sister to help you out with minor things? Why not just hire a service?"

"I thought she was broke. I mean, like destitute broke. I've been to her house. Well, I might not have been, but she would take me there. All she did was complain about how there were leaks in the plumbing. Rats everywhere. Once when I was there, something brushed up against me, and I had nightmares for a month about her getting eaten alive. Now when I think of the things she said and did to me, I'm all the more hurt by them." Tabby told her she was sorry. "Not as sorry as she's going to be when I find her. I'm not going to let her get by with any of the shit she's been pulling on me."

"Good for you." She smiled in the direction that Joey had spoken to her from. "Mr. and Mrs. Anderson are here. They're Caleb's grandparents. They're very nice people. They're going to see what sort of help they can do for you. I guess Mr. Anderson, Sheppard, has been studying up on law and said he can help if you'd allow him. Or he'd do it anyway if you didn't. He's a funny man."

"I'll take what I can get."

She heard the crunch of gravel and wondered if that was them. When someone rang the doorbell, Yasmine tensed up her body for news that her sister had found her. As soon as she heard the voices in the hallway, she knew she was about to meet the Andersons.

Joey led her into the hallway, where the voices were louder and introduced her to the elderly couple. She'd not been using her cane as much so she could get the layout of the rooms at Caleb's home. The one that Joey had purchased was still devoid of furniture, but he was working on that.

The hug she got from the mister was just what she needed. She might have held onto him for just a little longer than necessary because he asked her if she was all right. Nodding, then shaking her head, it took the other three to explain to him what she'd dealt with today. Another hug, then one from his wife, was all it took for her to start crying again.

"I'm so sorry. It's been a great deal of learning today." Melissa, who insisted she call the elderly grandma that, said she'd have been a basket case. "I think I am. When I found out…well, it's been a lot of harsh realities I had no idea about."

They all retired, as Sheppard called it, to the living room, where tea was brought in by their butler and served. Usually, Yasmine didn't like to drink hot beverages around others, as she had always been told she was a slob. But Joey not only put a napkin on her lap, but he helped her line up the handle so she could drink it without any trouble.

While Caleb and Joey brought the other couple up to date, Yasmine paid more attention this time. It wasn't nearly as painful to hear it this time, as she felt like she had a family around her. There wasn't, not really, but she was feeling about as safe as she'd been in a very long time.

"Yasmine, what can you tell us about your sister? Something that isn't in this file. Do you have a sense that she's always been this way? Manipulative and cruel?" Yasmine told Melissa she hadn't realized it until this, but she had been. "Do you believe it was jealousy? Of you being blind and getting extra attention?"

She thought about that. Was she? Some of the things her sister had said to her as her sight was fading seemed to surface now. Yasmine handed her cup and saucer to Joey and leaned back on the couch.

"The day I was told I was going to be blind before I was ten had me, as you can imagine, not believing them. The doctor had given my mom a bunch of pamphlets that told her what to expect, and I remember Jazzie taking them from her. Snatched them, I guess. The nurse in the room with us took them from Jazzie, and I remember thinking at the time that Jazzie wasn't going to like that." She thought about the newspaper article that had appeared in the paper a couple of days later and told them about it. "I think now—maybe even back then a little—that Jazzie hurt the nurse. Actually, killed her. Her name was Merriam Lancaster. I'm a little fuzzy on the details of her death, but it was horrific, I know. But I think it was a fall. Down a flight of stairs at her apartment complex. I remember thinking that she lived on the bottom floor, so why would she have been falling from the top level to the very bottom floor?"

"She fell down six flights of stairs. It says here in the article that her back was broken, leaving her paralyzed from the neck down. The police speculate that she might have been pushed, as it seemed impossible for her to have fallen so far, but that's all it talks about regarding looking into it." Joey paused as he spoke about the article. "Her head had been brutalized badly, but according to the article, they weren't sure if it was from the fall or something else. Mrs. Lancaster was removed from life support four days after the accident. There hasn't been anyone arrested in the case, according to an article that came out a few years ago about cold cases. Her death certificate lists her cause of death as blunt force trauma, and there are no notes on whether it was caused by accident, suicide, or homicide. But there was an autopsy performed. I wonder what we'd find if we were to pull that from the archives." Yasmine asked Joey if Merriam's body had been cremated or buried. "Let me see. Buried. I don't know what we could find out if we were to exhume the body, but it's worth a shot. Perhaps we'll put that to an attorney when we get that far."

"That sounds like a good plan."

She heard the crunch of gravel and alerted the people with her that they had company coming. When someone left the room, she knew it was Caleb. He was the only man she knew that wore Old Spice. It smelled really good on him, but she did wonder how he was able to get the old-fashioned scent after so long. Or did they still make it?

"Hello." Joey stood her up and guided her across the room, pointing out places that might trip her up. Her heart was still pounding when she heard Jazzie's voice talking to Caleb. "What can I do for you? However, if you're selling something, I don't want it."

"I'm looking for my sister. I was told that she lives around here. I want you to bring her to me." Caleb told her that no one would have told her that. "Of course they did. Are you calling me a liar?"

"I am, as a matter of fact. There isn't anyone in this town that would tell you shit. So how did you happen to come around to this house? Or have you been going to every house in this town?" Caleb laughed. "So, you have been annoying the good people of this town looking for your supposed sister."

"I do have a sister. She's a cripple and needs to take her medication." Joey asked Yasmine if she was on any meds. Shaking her head, she felt him leave her there. "You? What the hell are you doing here?"

"I'm his brother. She came to our house earlier today and accused me of having her sister. I had to threaten the police being called to get her out of my hair. Now she's here bothering you." She didn't know what was going on during the silences, and it bothered her a little. "If I were you, I'd call them now. Especially since she's been going around town calling her handicapped sister a cripple to anyone that gets within ear shot of her."

"Why is the first thing someone wants to do is call the police? Christ, I just want to get her back to her home so I can put her under lock and key. When she wanders off like this, there is no telling what sort of things could happen to her. She's a cripple, as I have pointed out several times already." Having enough, Yasmine walked around the wall she'd been hiding behind and knew the exact moment Jazzie saw her. "There you are. I thought you told me she wasn't here. Morons. Come on, Yazzie. Let's get home and forget the trouble you caused me. I have no idea who would have let you out of the hospital when I left explicit instructions for you not to have visitors. Come on now."

"No, I'm happy where I am." She felt Joey's arm go around her and felt much stronger for it. "This is Joey Phillips. We're going to be living here and perhaps someday getting married. I'm not going anywhere with you. I don't need you to keep me under lock and key. I'm not going to let you make me feel like a cripple either. Also, I don't take any meds that would require you to chase me all over this town, making a fool of yourself by telling people that. Jazzie, were you ever a nice person?"

~*~

Jazzie wasn't happy. After the police had arrived at Mr. Anderson's home, she was escorted off the property. As she was driving down the road, thinking about how she was going to have to come back at a later time, the officer behind her turned on his lights. Tempted to race off, knowing her car was much faster than his, another cruiser blocked her way. Five officers got out of their cruisers, hands on their guns, and approached her.

"Ms. Dennis, you had best think on bothering people around here for much longer. It's come to our attention that you've been making a right nuisance of yourself since you arrived four days ago. You should take this time to reflect on how badly you wish to be run out of town or simply arrested." She told the officer she'd been caring for her sister all her life. "Well, it seems to me and the boys here, not to mention Joey, that she's just fine on her own. They're a nice couple, don't you think?"

"No, I don't think so. What I can tell you is that she's not right in the head. Stupid, I think it was the doctors called her. Being blind has affected her mental health." The officer, his name tag only referred to him as Kimble, asked her if she was the one affecting her mental health. "What a thing to say to me. I'll have you know that she can't function on her own. Why, every time I go to her little shack of a place, she's been banged up."

"You mean like what happened to her to have her ending up in the hospital? Yes, ma'am, we're looking into that too. We have a buddy of Joey's that is helping us with that by us being able to call on the Feds anytime we want. Why, it'll surprise you to know that Caleb told me he was thinking of exhuming a woman by the name of Merriam Lancaster." Jazzie didn't blink. Nor did she bother asking who the person was. "I can see by the look on your face that you're familiar with that name. Well, it's going to come to light soon. Also, the murder of those nice people at the bank. Did you happen to know anything about that?"

"I haven't any idea what you're going on about. I came here to get my sister and to take her home. Nothing more. If you're going to dig up dead women after twelve years, then that is nothing to me." He pointed out that he'd not said how long it had been. "So? Do you think I'd not heard of the woman? Or didn't know that she was the nurse to my little sister? Christ man, stop watching all those crime shows and help me get my sister from the clutches of those men. There is no telling how they're treating her when I'm not around."

"Now, that would be you treating her badly and not Joey, the man she's going to be marrying." She'd see about that and nearly told the man but held her tongue. Too much information, as the saying goes, was too many things to keep track of when caught in a lie. "Now, you head on down the road and right out of our town. If I see you here again, Ms. Dennis, I will have you arrested. I don't really need a reason for arresting you, but I got myself one. Annoying the crap out of everyone you meet. You have a good day now."

Getting to the outskirts of town took every bit of her patience. The police followed her, each of them using their lights and sirens to make sure anyone within hearing distance knew she was being escorted out of town. Fucking bastards. As soon as they peeled away from her car, she pulled over to the side of the road, got out of her car, and screamed as loudly as she could.

Picking up a stick that was lying on the ground in front of her, she beat a tree with it. She was feeling better until a small piece of either the tree or the branch came back and slammed her right in the head. Falling back, she felt her head crack as it hit something.

When she woke, she was chained to a bed. Jazzie was sure she had ended up in the morgue— everything around her was a sickly shade of gray.

A nurse came into the room with her just as she was jerking on the handcuffs and told her that she was in Mercy. She'd been found on the side of the road.

"Who found me? I demand to know." The nurse tisked at her. "Damn it, is everyone around here stupid?"

"I'd say that's a horrible way to get on the good side of someone. My name is Richard Jamison. I'm an FBI agent for the United States government." She told him la-de-da. "I was told you were combative. Anyway, I'm here to inform you that your car was stolen. As well as anything you might have had in it when you were found."

"I have insurance." She looked at the man when he made an audible sound. "What? You think I should be upset more? I'm not. As I said, I have insurance, as well as a LoJack on it. As soon as I get my phone, I'll be able to get it back."

"You didn't have a phone when you came in here." That had her cursing up a blue streak, as her dad used to say. "Precisely. When you were brought in, you were very combative, I was told. That is why you're cuffed to the bed. If you're willing to behave yourself, I'll have them removed."

"Are you here to help me with whatever had anyone call you in, or is this how you get your jollies? I don't know if you're aware of this or not, but I've had a really shitty day." He said he was there to make sure she understood the rules regarding the Andersons, as well as Joey and Yasmine. "Yasmine is my sister. I've been caring for her since we were children. I'm going to continue to do so until such time that she dies."

"You should have said until one of us dies. It wouldn't make you sound like you might be hurrying her death along. But we're not worried about you getting to her any longer. She's been set up with a team of men and women that would give their lives for her to be safe. That goes for the rest of the aforementioned people." Jazzie just stared at him. "I'm also to tell you—or inform, however you wish to look at it—that you are not to be within ten feet of any of the people I mentioned. After seeing your performance when you were brought in, I can see why they kept you away."

"Are you finished yet?" He shook his head. "Then get it over with. I have shit that I have to take care of, one of them being my sister. I guess I'm going to have to have her committed or something. They're brainwashing her or some shit."

"It's funny you should say that." He handed her a sheet of paper. "That is a certification from a firm that I work with that states your sister isn't having any issues that would require you, as her family, or anyone else for that matter, to keep tabs on her. She doesn't take any kind of impairment medications. She's fit to live on her own and hold down a job. All of which she's been doing very well at since you've been cut out of her life. Oh yes, that's another thing. She has cut you out of her life. You are no longer her next of kin on any of her insurance policies. You're not going to be welcome at her wedding, nor will you be allowed to be around any children she and Joey might have."

"Yazzie? To have children? Are you insane? She's a cripple, for heaven's sake! My sister can't even take care of herself, much less a child. Surely no one is going to allow her to keep a child of hers. She has enough trouble just keeping herself from falling on her face all the time." Mr. Jamison then told her that Yazzie was looking for her two children. Her breathing caught in her throat. She knew her face was giving her away, but there wasn't anything she could have done about it. Jazzie, for the first time in her life, didn't have a quick comeback to someone. When she could finally speak, knowing the damage had been done, she glared at the man. "I don't have any children. Now, if you have nothing more to say, I want out of this contraption and out of this hospital. As I said, I have things to do."

It took her another two hours before she was released to go. One of the officers took her to her hotel and made sure she was inside before he left. They had told her that she had nineteen stitches in her forehead, as well as some other cuts on her cheek. There would be hell to pay if there was any scarring, she told the staff. All that earned her was them laughing at her. Jazzie had a good mind to forget about her sister and move on. But there was just too much depending on Yazzie being with her.

Taking a nice long soak in the provided tub, she was glad to see the back side of that town for now. Deciding that she needed a nice dinner with some wine, a box of chocolates, as well as a good fuck, she wished that she had her phone. It had a list of fuckable men that she could have called. She hadn't any idea if there was such a thing as a good fuck around here, but she was willing to pay whatever it took to get her rocks off. Her sister, however, was going to be a problem.

Yazzie had always been so easy to fool. Even before she'd been blind, Jazzie could get her into trouble easily. But after she was completely without sight, it was so much better. Like the bank robberies.

It had taken her nearly getting caught for her to come up with the plan to use her sister as bait. It hadn't even been her idea. The police had shown up at her sister's apartment once and questioned her about her role in a robbery. Once it was pointed out that she was blind and unable to drive the car she'd been in, Jazzie began to watch her sister's movements closer. The way she wore her hair and clothing. Now she could afford a wig that was a match to Yazzie's hair style, a simple ponytail that hung down her back. However, if this shit with her and that man kept up, Jazzie didn't know what she was supposed to do.

Jazzie had been committing crimes since she'd been old enough to figure out that it paid well. She'd been nine when she'd robbed her first place. Nine and a half when she'd killed the first time. Lancaster had been her third murder. Dragging her down each and every step by her hair had been the greatest payback to someone since, and even before.

Remembering to call her cell phone provider before she left her room, Jazzie was seven kinds of pissed when she finally hung up on them. The man who was "helping" her told her she'd have to wait until she had her account number before they could get her something to use in the meantime.

Everything she needed was in that phone. Addresses. Calendars. Even bank schedules. She could only hope that whoever took it didn't know what the hell they were looking at. Anyone in that town wouldn't have known, if they found it, what was on it. They were all inbred, she thought and didn't have a single brain cell to think beyond their next meal or fuck. Jazzie hated small towns and the people that lived in them.

Going out seemed to be her only option in getting in a better mood. According to the phone book — why they had one was beyond her, it only had ten pages — there were as many as four bars in town. All of them served a meal and bar food. So long as she could get herself a steak and potato, Yazzie would be all right with that. Leaving the hotel, she realized she could walk to all four of the places she had to choose from. One point in the favor of the little town, she thought with a giggle.

Getting back to her hotel around midnight, Jazzie ignored the front desk personnel when they said her name. She was exhausted, unhappy with the turn of events while out and what she'd been able to not find out about Yazzie.

"Ms. Dennis, I'm sorry to tell you this, but your car has been found." She asked him if it could wait until in the morning. "Yes, I can do that. Don't you want to know what's happened to it?"

"No. No, I fucking don't. Tell me tomorrow. Or don't. I could give a shit about it right now. I'm going to bed. If anyone comes to the door before I call down here, they'll be dead. Do I make myself clear?" The man nodded. "Good. Don't disturb me for any reason."

"Yes, ma'am."

As she rode the elevator up, she did have a moment of wonder about her car but brushed it off as soon as she entered her suite and fell naked into her bed.

Chapter 4

Standing at the deck door that led out to the back yard, Joey sipped his tea as he contemplated his life now. It boggled his mind that only a few weeks ago, he'd been sitting under a bridge with a bunch of other homeless and broken men, with a gun in his hands. He'd been more than broken, he thought with a grimace. Joey had thought it was the only way to finish what had started out as a small break in a bridge to ending his life because he'd thought that was it.

He could still see the look on Tabby's face when she took the gun from him, pointed it at his head, and asked him if he wanted her to kill him. He didn't remember her even reaching for it, but had it she did.

After putting it on her person, she got up and made him do the same as they handed out blankets and warm food to the others around him that night.

For taking him into their home, Joey would be forever grateful. There was no doubt to him that they had saved his life. Because if he'd not succeeded that night in pulling the trigger, he would have eventually and would have never met Yasmine.

Tabby and Caleb had been helping him ever since, being true to their word in treating him as Caleb's brother and nothing else. They'd given him not just a hand up but also a hand in all aspects of his life. Now he had, because of them, Yasmine in his life.

Joey had come to depend a great deal on the skills he'd had as an officer in the service. Mostly it was describing events, people, and furniture. Yesterday he and Yasmine had gone furniture shopping. It was a great deal more fun than he'd thought it should have been.

Yasmine would sit on whatever they were searching for in the way of comfortable furniture, and it was his job to tell her what it looked like. Texture she had. It was colors, though she still remembered them from childhood, that he had to explain to her. Patterns were tougher for him.

"It has scribbles on it. In neat lines." She asked him to do better. "I don't know. Scribbles of brown and tan going in different directions. Like maybe a kid would do coloring on the wall and moving around."

"Okay, that helps." He had cocked his brow at her and remembered she couldn't see him. "So the pattern is in squares or just random?"

"Squares. I can see them now. I don't know if I like it. The scribbles are too close, and when I move my head, they sort of look like one of those circles that they use to hypnotize you." Yasmine got up and asked him where the next one was. "You're all right with me not liking it for that reason?"

"Well, it's not like it's going to make me dizzy if I look at it. Nor put me to sleep. Where is the next one?" They avoided things with patterns that were too much for him. "I used to like earth tones. I can do bright too. Like I said, it won't bother me, but I want guests to feel less like they've stepped into a painting of a five-year-old and more of a comfy place to have a conversation."

By the time they were finished with getting what they needed and were having dinner, they were both so exhausted they decided to stay in town for the night. Getting them separate rooms that adjoined, he thought that when he made love to Yasmine for the first time, he wanted it to be in their own home. He told her that too.

"I'd like that. I don't have a lot of experience with sex. Men in general, for that matter. I've lived a sheltered life up until now, and while I would like to blame it all on my sister, I didn't fight her overly much about not dating. I guess I was more afraid than I ever thought I was. Like crippling fear. Not that it makes me a cripple, but just very afraid of the world around me." He told her he could understand that. "Good. Let's get a good night's sleep and go home tomorrow."

So here he was, up at the butt crack of dawn, waiting for the furniture to arrive. Laughing to himself, he decided there could be worse things in life. Like he could be still living under a bridge or dead. His cell phone rang just as he was laughing again.

"Joey, it's Sher. I was wondering if you could

come down to the station. We have an issue with that woman again that I could use your help with." He asked if she'd hurt anyone. "No. But she's telling me that you hurt her. I don't see anything, but she is getting louder and louder about how you're also a degenerate, taking advantage of her crippled sister — she sure does like that word, doesn't she? I'm telling you right now, Joey, if you'd marry that girl, I think that would set her ass on fire. But if you could, come on down here and set this woman straight, though I'm not sure that'll help. She sure does have it bad for having her sister coming back to live with her."

"I've been thinking on that too. I'll talk to you when I get her out of your hair." Sher told him he'd appreciate that. "All right. Yasmine is out with Tabby, so I'll tell her where I'm going — damn it. I have furniture coming in. Let me call you back."

After talking to Caleb, he found out the women were at his house. Tabby was going to come here with Yasmine and wait on the stuff coming in. Since they'd figured out what went where it was a simple thing to have the furniture company put it in the right room. Caleb said he'd help him move it around when he was back.

On his way to the station house, he thought about the things he'd been thinking about that morning. How Jazmine wanted her sister home. He knew she wanted, or perhaps needed, to control her, but he thought it was more than likely something to do with a robbery. He'd been looking into unsolved robberies for the last five years, and the same MO was used on each of the nine of them.

The woman was in charge. She was brazen about showing her face and hair. So were the men that were with her but to a lesser degree. Also, the men she would bring with her ended up being found dead a few days later.

Then there was his theory about how Yasmine had ended up beaten. Yasmine told him she'd mentioned to her sister about moving back to the blind college and becoming a teacher there. A life skills helper, so to speak. Jazzie, Yasmine told her, wasn't thrilled about her moving to the secluded compound, but she said they'd discuss it over dinner. After drugging her, he thought, she'd had her sister beaten up so she'd be hurt enough to either stay put or — and he was sure the second part was truer to what was happening — Yasmine would move in with her sister, and all would be right with her world. How that was supposed to work, he had no idea, but then, he didn't delve into the mind of crazy bitches all that often.

Pulling into the station parking lot, he got out quickly. There were other officers hanging out, all of them standing on the steps to the police station, and he wondered about that. As soon as he entered the massive old building, he decided he wanted to join them. The place was loud with angry voices. So much so that he put his fingers into his mouth and let go of a shrill whistle that had everything stop.

"Now, we're going to do this calmly and without you getting all shitty with people." When Jazmine started for him, he simply pulled out his gun and held it at his side. "You come any closer to me, and I will shoot you. I'd say in the head, but I doubt very much you have anything up there other than dust bunnies. Now sit the fuck down and shut that fucking pie hole of yours."

"Excuse me." Joey told Jazmine no, he wasn't excusing her at all. "You can't talk to me like that. I'll have you know that I'm not going to put up with your shit either."

"Good, then we're both on the same page. What the hell are you doing back here in town? I thought you were told not to come here again." She told him her sister was being held against her will. "Do you by chance have another sister that we don't know about, Jazmine? Because if you're meaning Yasmine, then that's not even close to being the truth, now is it? She and I bought furniture together. We also looked at rings. I'm going to marry her as soon as the paperwork is—"

"She doesn't have my permission." He laughed with the other men in the room with them. "You're not going to marry her because I say who she sees and dates. And that isn't going to be you. As soon as I'm allowed to talk to her, you'll see that she'll side with me."

"Will she? You mean like she did the day you came out to my brother's house and demanded that we bring out the cripple to you? Or are you talking about when you first arrived to take her home? I think she ended up at my brother's house too." Joey laughed at the expression on her face. "I don't know about you, but it sounds to me like Yasmine doesn't want to have shit to do with you. I would have thought the first time she snuck away in the middle of the night would have given you a clue. You must be about as dense as a piece of tofu."

"You monster." She turned to the captain that was still standing behind her. "Did you hear what he called me? He called me a monster."

"Nah, he called you tofu. It's bean curd made by soy milk. My wife and I, we have it twice a week. My favorite is— Well, I can see by that pinched look on your face you don't care about how to cook it. However, he didn't call you a monster. You're more of a pain in the flipping ass. However, he didn't call you that." She asked him if he had called her one. "No. I was being polite, more than you were, and called you a pain. Which you have been. And I'll freely admit it. Anyone that comes in here spouting off lies like you have since you got here is a pain. Taking up the time of officers for your nonsense claims against the Anderson men. My goodness, woman, give it up. Yasmine is a grown woman that votes and everything. Why don't you just go home and behave yourself? Or do you have a motive for wanting her under your thumb?" The captain looked at him and winked. "Joey, before I forget to tell you,

I've got all the forms needed to exhume those bodies you and Caleb came in here asking about. There wasn't a lick of trouble about them either. The Feds are sure—"

"What the hell are you talking about now? Exhuming bodies? Why on earth would you be doing something like that when there are real crimes being done right here? My sister is going to come home with me, or else I will have your job." He handed her his badge, and Jazmine stepped back from it so quickly that Joey erupted in laughter. "What the hell do you think is so funny, moron? Do you think I couldn't do his job and yours? Well, I'm a smart woman who knows the law more than I'm betting either of you do."

"I'm sure you do, Jazmine. That way, you can keep track of all the crimes you're doing and the number of years you'll spend in prison once we can tag you to some of the unsolved crimes, such as bank robberies and the murder of at least twenty-seven people that were in those banks. Including the men you hired right off the street to help you with the robberies." Sher didn't stop there. "Then there is the beating of your sister, Yasmine. Threatening an officer. Car theft. Christ, you have a longer rap sheet than most mobsters. And you're going to be tried on every one of them too."

Joey was glad he'd been looking right at Jazmine, or he might have missed the look on her face. He'd been a cop long enough that he knew that look better than most. It told him that Sher had shocked her. That he was getting too close to whatever she was hiding. It also made him realize that he was indeed on the right track with what was going on.

"I haven't any idea what you're talking about." Her reply was too late in coming like she had needed to think about what he was saying and realized she needed to make some kind of token answer. Putting his gun away, he turned when the door behind him opened. "There you are, Yazzie. I've been trying to reach you for days. Where the hell did you lay down your phone? I'm going to get you one of those pagers so you can find things when you lay them down and are not able to find them. This is why you can't have children. I'm sure that would be—"

"Oh, do shut up, Jazmine." Yasmine reached out her hand, and he took it, bringing her closer to him. "I want to clear up a few things with you, Jazmine, right now. First of all, I'm not now nor ever going back home with you. In the event that you've lost your mind at some point—which to anyone around you it certainly seems possible—I'm not going to live with you. Also, *when* I decide to have a child, which will be my choice, a baby makes noises when they need something from their mother, so it's doubtful I'd lose one. You should know this from your own children. Oh, I forgot, you sold them off. Your son is dead, by the way. The daughter, my niece, is going to be found, and I'll bring her to live with us, as my daughter. Luckily for me and her, I have friends in very high places to help with this search. Also, I just spoke to you two days ago, and I told you then that I wasn't going to do anything with you or for you. Which I'm thinking has to do with another bank robbery. I just don't understand why you'd think ignoring what I say is going to make me do what you want. I'm a grown assed woman, Jazmine, and I can take care of my fucking self. Get over it, or else. And yes, that was a threat. Try me, and you'll see what I can do to you."

Again, he was glad he'd been looking at Jazmine, or he would have missed the flash of anger, as well as a bit of fear on her face. In a flat second, however, rage took over. As soon as she took one step forward, he pushed Yasmine behind him and drew his gun again.

"Don't. Or do it, and we'll end this right now." She glared, a hatred so hot that it surpassed the anger she'd had just seconds ago. "Get out of town. Out of our life, or I won't hesitate to shoot you. You've been warned, several times, that you're not welcome here. Neither are you welcome in our lives. Leave now, while you still have a bit of freedom left to take care of your personal matters. When I'm finished with you, it's doubtful that you'll be able to ever see the light of day again."

Without a word, she started for the door. He moved so that Yasmine was still behind him. When Jazmine got to the door, she turned to them. Joey didn't know what to expect, but he was going to be ready for it.

"Are you coming back with me, Yazzie? I'm your sister, and you owe me." Yasmine told her no, she wasn't. "You'll regret that. Both of you will. I'm not saying that I'm giving up—I'm not—but you'll both come to regret doing this to me."

Then she left them standing there. It wasn't until Yasmine touched his arm that he let out the breath he'd not realized he'd been holding. Joey felt as if he'd run a marathon. Twice.

~*~

"The furniture is at home. Tabby said we did well in picking it out." Joey asked her if she was all right. "No. And I don't want to talk about anything about my sister just yet. The lamps are beautiful, I was told, but one of them was broken. The company that brought the stuff said they'd return it to the store and have another brought out to us. What did she mean when she said we'd regret doing this to her?"

"I don't know." She nodded and prattled on about other things that had happened to her today. "You're babbling. I know you're aware of that, but I'd like to point out that I'm a little frightened as well. Also, I have some things to tell you about what happened when you're ready to talk about it."

"I don't know that I ever will, to be honest." Joey asked her about the little girl. "She's really on her way here. I don't know anything about her other than what Caleb told me. Having money sure does get people doing what you want them to do, doesn't it?"

"I'd say it does. How do you know this is your sister's daughter?" Yasmine told him that Caleb had taken a swab of her DNA to a detective friend of his. "Okay. So he had enough of a match to know she's our niece. Are we going to be adopting her?"

"I meant to talk to you about it before I went and said that to Jazmine. I don't even want to refer to her as my sister anymore. The little girl is six years old. Blonde and blue eyed. Caleb has a picture of her, but I, of course, am only going on what Tabby told me. Why would she sell off her own children?" Again he told her that he didn't know. "I know that. But I can't imagine someone thinking to discard a child is something that is all right. The little boy, his name was Jacobson, died when he was just barely two. Caleb said it was ruled an accident, but the way he said it has me thinking he's not so sure about that. Oh, the little girl, her name is Madison. If they've shortened it, I have no idea. She's been in foster care since the people who took her decided that once they had children of their own, they no longer had any use for her. No use for her. Like she's a piece of furniture that is taking up too much room in your home."

"What else do you know about her? I'm sure that if Caleb gave you so little, you would have beaten him for more information." Yasmine smiled, and it felt a little better. "I knew you were holding back on me. I need that smile as much as I do you, love."

"Madison is six, as I said. She's been in the system for some time now. Jazmine didn't sell her off so much as she had someone else do it. That person sold her to an undercover cop, and she was saved that way. Jacobson, her twin, wasn't so lucky." He told her he was sorry. "So am I. The two of them would have been six now. The people she sold him to were all right at first, I guess. They were wealthy and full of themselves. According to the reports that Caleb got, they would bring him out when they had people over to show him off. He took a tumble down a flight of stairs one night when his parents weren't home. I'm beginning to think Jazmine has a thing for killing people on stairs. The reason I say that is because several of the men that were in on a robbery were found in a stairwell of an abandoned building. I don't know that she was involved in Jacobson's death, but at this point, who the hell knows. I'm just babbling. I'm nervous, and I do that sometimes."

Yasmine knew they were home when Joey stopped the car and turned off the motor. But neither of them moved to get out of the car. If she was honest with herself, she was heartbroken. And afraid. Afraid that Joey would think she was too much trouble and be done with her.

"I don't know what you're thinking, but I'm sure it's not about how beautifully Madison is going to fit into our lives. Our, Yasmine. Not anyone else but ours." Turning her face toward him, she wished that she could see his expression. "Our license has been filed to say we're married. Caleb did his marriage to Tabby the same way. No big deal, it was finished. Anytime you say, we can get married with all the pomp you want. Just say the word."

She didn't have to even think about it. "I'm happy with things just like they are. So long as you call me Mrs. Phillips for the first time." He did so and then kissed her. "I love you, Joey. So much so that it's just too much sometimes the amount that I feel for you."

"I love you as well, my darling wife. How about we go inside, make love for the rest of the day, and have a midnight snack when we get hungry?" Joey started cursing when she asked him about Caleb. "I forgot he was here. All right. As soon as he leaves, the two of us will fuck each other nearly stupid."

He got out of the car first and came around to her side to help her out. Taking her cane from her, he folded it up and told her what sort of things he was planning to do to her. Before she was on the first step of their front decking, she was about as needy as she'd been in her life.

"Caleb, let's get this going, shall we? I'd like to be able to sit on my own stuff one night soon and invite people over to do the same." Caleb told him he was the one that was wasting time. "Good point. All right, let's begin in the living room."

They moved furniture around the living room for over an hour. She had to have space between the larger pieces and smaller ones, such as a footstool needed to be close to something larger. Joey didn't care if she used her cane at home, but she wanted to not have to search for it if she were to leave it someplace in the house. He had gotten her a beeper that she could put on it, and that was great when she was ready to leave the house.

Joey had also purchased her an audio plan so she could listen to books rather than reading them. Yasmine had never thought of doing that before and found that she enjoyed it a great deal. Like when she was on the deck enjoying the sun. Waiting for her appointment with the doctor. All sorts of things were there for her to enjoy with the way the reader would weave a story for her, using their voice to convey anger or happiness.

The doorbell ringing while she was in the living room startled her a little. Joey and Caleb had taken the broken down cardboard out to the recycling bins, and it was just her and Tabby in the house. Telling her not to answer the door, they looked at the camera that had only been set up that morning by Caleb's company.

"It's Jazzie. She has flowers in her hand like she wants to give them to you to make amends. Like anyone would believe that." Yasmine giggled with her friend. "Anyway, we'll let Joey handle her. She seems to be the most afraid of him."

Joey handled it by calling the police, which really pissed Jazzie off when they dragged her away. She even managed to hit the officers with her flowers, and that was when a long-bladed knife fell out onto the ground. She was cursing and spitting. It might have been funny had Yasmine been able to see it for herself, but the others did a fantastic job in making sure she could almost see all her sister's antics. Jazzie wasn't going to give up, it seemed.

Perhaps now that she was in a jail cell for a few days, Yasmine would go and see her. Try to figure her out. The evidence that was being found about her was mounting up, and Yasmine couldn't make herself feel bad for Jazzie. She'd made her bed, taking Yasmine through the sheets with her, and she was going to have to pay. Good riddance, Yasmine thought.

The firm she worked for, the government office of the National Security Agency, or NSA for short, was going to come and set up her computers for her to work again. Since she worked on sensitive things, they needed to make sure she had a secure network, as well as all the braille equipment she would need to work. It was a job she could do at home, and it paid very well. Benefits were fantastic as well.

Yasmine had been told by Joey that she didn't need to work. But after explaining to him why she needed to, he agreed with her. Since Caleb had found him and had been helping him financially, he'd been learning a great deal about wealth and how to invest so that he and Jasmine would have money for kids and their golden years.

It had been a long day, she thought, before heading upstairs. So while it ended on a nice note, with them having furniture and Jazzie being arrested again, she was worried about the next few days. Whatever happened was going to happen, she supposed.

By the time Caleb and Tabby left, she and Joey both were so exhausted that they barely made it to the bedroom before they were asleep on their feet. Getting into bed had never felt so good. Tomorrow, she thought, was going to be a fresh day.

Chapter 5

Joey hated being called away this morning. He didn't mind the work, but he had hoped to wake his new wife up by making sure she knew she was his. But duty called. It sucked, but he was there for the police force when they needed him.

The body that had been found hadn't been there very long. It was still decomposing, and the shorts and shirt she had on were intact enough that he could tell it was a female victim. Her purse and a pair of hiking boots were atop her body. They were waiting for the coroner to come out and take his pictures before either of them touched anything. The female's purse was lying right on top of her body, covered in blood.

He and Sher had cordoned off the area first thing after they arrived on the scene. Sher was asking questions of the man, Mr. Benson, who had uncovered the gruesome mess, while Joey inspected the area around the dig sight. Mr. Benson's dog, Mary Beth, had brought him back one of the femur bones after not finding the stick he'd thrown.

"I never in my life expected to see this sort of thing out here. Why, you could have knocked me over with a feather. It did. Knock me back. It took my head a bit for it to let my eyes tell me that was a body right there." Mr. Benson shook his head. "That ain't right, you know. Just putting a body out in the open like it was. I guess they thought that putting that there wagon over it might have protected it a bit. But that still don't make it right. What they should have done was call on you cops. Damned shame that people have no respect for the dead no more."

"Yes, sir. Do you know who owns this land?" Joey knew it was Mr. Benson, but Sher was asking to make sure he wouldn't lie to them. The elderly man said that his son, also Mr. Ed Benson, had bought it from him a couple of weeks ago. "All right. Do you know where your son might be? I just have a few questions about the land here. You know, if he has security cameras and the like. It might go a long way in us being able to find whoever it was that killed this poor woman."

"He don't have nothing like that. Wanted me to give him the land, on account'a him being my son, but a man's gotta eat. Besides, I don't like him overly much anymore. Took all of his savings, or what he said was his, to buy me out. 'Course, he didn't have any savings either that I ever heard of, but he surely did come up with the cash money." Ed laughed a little. "I have cameras around here. Right over there on the barn, as a matter of fact. I don't know that I've checked on the recordings in a while, but you're more than welcome to have a look at them. They're saved up on that there cloud thing, so they'll be a lot to look over."

Joey could have kissed the man. As Sher was walking back to the cruiser, which was what the two of them had come in, Ed stopped walking and looked at Sher and himself. Joey was just close enough to them that he heard the two of them talking. He was going to have one of the deputies go over to the house and get whatever was needed to look over the films if the older man didn't want to go. Mr. Benson looked like a man that had a secret he was about to share.

"Whatever you have to tell us, Mr. Benson, will go a long way in finding out who this woman is. I'm sure her parents would like to bring her home to rest in peace." He nodded, then pulled out the most pristine handkerchief he'd ever seen and blew his nose. "Do you have an idea who might have done this?"

"I know that pretty little purse she had on her. I think it's one of the ones I gave a girl once when she admired it. My wife, you know, is gone, so it didn't hurt none to give it over to her. I'm thinking that her name is Lily Anne Manor. She is…was a little bitty thing that used to come around the house to help me out with some little cleaning up." He blew his nose again. "I'm thinking, and please don't be thinking badly of me, but I'm thinking that my son did this thing. He'd been chasing after her for some time now, and she finally had to have her daddy have a talk with him. I don't know how that turned out, but she ain't been around for a couple of weeks."

"All right, Mr. Benson. You and I will head

over to your house now and see to those recordings. If it was your son, you know he's going to have to be arrested." He nodded, then looked at Joey before turning back to Sher. "Something else?"

"He won't come to you easy. I know that Joey here, he can knock a penny out of a bird's mouth without touching the bird with his shooting. Might be best if you were to let him take me home. I like you, Sher. I surely do. But Ed, he's a bastard, and you might have to have some fancy shooting going on before it ends." Joey waited on Sher to make the decision. He was only there to assist. It was his call. "I'm telling you right now, Sher, I will not bail him out. I won't go and see him. He's done with me if he's the one that did this to little Lily Anne."

Sher was going to wait on the coroner while Joey took Mr. Benson to his home. The man cried off and on while they drove the short distance. Joey felt sorry for him. There wasn't anything he could say to the man until they were sure it was Ed Junior.

Setting him up with the password and sign-in, Mr. Benson went out on the deck to drink a beer. He offered Joey one, which he turned down, and the man walked out onto the deck. As soon as Joey pulled up the camera, he could see that the coroner had arrived and was taking pictures. There was audio as well.

Pulling on the set of headphones next to the computer, he could hear Sher asking questions. After the purse was photographed, it was opened. The camera Sher was using was out of date, and Joey thought about purchasing the station a new one for things such as this. It would look better in the courtroom if they were taking things like this seriously. Going to the file that was from three weeks ago, he started looking over the recordings.

Watching it on fast forward, it was funny to watch the sun rise in the sky only to be gone at the end of a couple of minutes. He also noted in his notes each time that the wagon hadn't been put over the shallow grave.

Just as he was ready to end the file, he saw some movement. He watched until the very end of the day, then started the one that started at midnight. He saw not just Ed Junior in the camera view, but another man too. They were arguing.

"I don't know why you don't just fucking pay me what you owe me, Ed. What the fuck did you think was going to happen when you 'borrowed' fifty grand off me? That I'd just blow it off because you're Ed Benson? Not fucking likely. Pay up or else. This is the third time you've not paid on time, and I'm fucking sick of carrying you. Do what you have to do, but get me that fucking money." Ed Junior simply pulled out a gun and shot the man in the head. The sound was so loud it startled Joey enough that he pulled the headphones off.

Pausing the recording to make note of the time and date, Joey's hands were shaking so badly that he could barely read his own handwriting. Putting down the pen in order to calm himself, Joey was afraid more than ever for Mr. Benson. If Ed Junior found out his dad had this, there was no telling what sort of death the older man would face. Backtracking a little on the recording, he wrote down the date and time in more legible writing.

As he watched, Ed Junior dragged the man into the barn and came out a few minutes later. When he went back in, it was nearly daylight out, and Joey had a feeling this was going to be a major dumping place for the man. Calling Sher on his cell phone, he told him another body was in the barn.

"Do you know who?" Joey told him he didn't

know but that Junior had owed the man fifty grand. "Well, we might be able to kill two birds with one stone on this and clean up a few files. I got me a lot of missing people. Joey, this entire area could be holding bodies. Find the girl yet?"

"I'm still looking. According to the date on this video, it was three weeks to the day ago. I'm just starting on the next file. Christ, Sher, I wonder how long he's been doing this." Sher said more than likely for a very long time. "I believe Mr. Benson is aware that this is his son and not just speculation that he did this. He's taking it hard."

"Mr. Benson is a good man. His wife was the best there was. Since she passed on, he's been walking around town a lot more with his dog. This isn't going to go well for him knowing for sure that his son is a murderer. Knowing the man the way I do, I'm sure he's going to think it's his fault in some way." Joey had a feeling, as Sher said, he'd figured it out already. "All right, we found the man. The bastard only put bails of hay over him to cover him up. I'm going to have to call in some help out here, Joey. This is bigger than our department can handle. You let me know about the girl or any other body you might be aware of."

He was going to have to have someone go over each and every file now to see if they could find other people that had the misfortune of being around Ed Junior. He had hoped that there would be only the two, but he was able to lead the team to five other people that Ed Junior had killed.

"I have him killing the girl. It was fourteen days ago. After raping her, he slit her throat before just leaving her where she lay. Then an hour later — it looks as if he might have showered because he has on different clothing — he simply tosses some hay over her body and moves the wagon over her. Christ, he's an animal, Sher. Nothing but a monster." Sher asked if there was any weapon. They'd not moved the body of Lily Anne yet, as they were looking for the bodies Joey was finding. "Under her body, I think. He did put something in the grave after moving the wagon again. I don't know what it might be, but we can assume, right?"

"Yes. The Feds are coming in. Caleb called them in for me. He called me because he couldn't get to you. Nothing is wrong, he assured me, but he is going to bring home his other brother and wanted to see if you wanted to go. I hope you don't mind, but I told him you're going to be busy for a while. He's going to go and get Yasmine for you and take her over to his house for a little while. He said that her and Tabby loved to hang out together. I didn't know that you two had more brothers."

"I'll explain it to you when I see you. It's complicated. And messy." Sher asked him if he thought what they were doing now wasn't the same. "I guess you're right. But this is a good story rather than death and mayhem. All right, I'm onto the next day. I hope to Christ we don't find anyone else."

Mr. Benson came in just as he was finishing up the call from Sher. He didn't say anything other than to ask if he'd found anything. After his nod to the older man, he sat down on the other chair in the little makeshift office.

"I've been thinking on a couple of things, Joey. I was wondering if you'd mind much if I stayed at your house for a couple of days. I…well, I'm not in a good set in my mind right now, and I don't think I'll be all right alone. You can tell me no. I'd understand it with you being newly married and all. But you're a good boy, and I'd—"

"I'll call my wife right now and have her set you up in one of the rooms. I'd love for you to stay with us. Even if you're not trying to chase away any demons, you're welcome to stay with us." He nodded and stood up. "Mr. Benson, you'll be all right. With what you've been able to give us, he'll not be able to get out of prison for a very long time."

"There was more than just the girl then." He told him yes. Joey didn't mention that there were as many of seven now. "I guess I could get into trouble for thinking he might be up to no good and not telling nary a soul about it."

"No. No one would even question you about it. And if they do, you can just say that he was your son, and no one will think badly of you for it." Mr. Benson thanked him. "You're welcome. The Feds are involved in this now. So as soon as they get here, I'll take you home. Pack up whatever you think you might need, and we'll head on over there after my replacement shows up. And bring Mary Beth with you. We have a nice fenced in back yard, so she'll be all right there too."

Joey called Yasmine, and she was all for the idea. After asking for a ride back to the house, she said that everything would be ready when they arrived. She even suggested having some lunch, as it was nearly noon now. Joey loved this woman.

It was an hour before they were able to leave. The man that had shown up to review the recordings needed to be set up. Joey didn't envy the man his task. There were as many as ten years' worth of days to review.

Yasmine was home, having had Caleb take her there to welcome Mr. Benson. Caleb was there, as well as Tabby, and the five of them had a nice lunch together. After he was shown his room, Ed asked if they'd mind if he had him a nice lying in for a bit. Everyone told him to do what he needed. As soon as he was gone, they all went to the living room.

Caleb asked what would happen to Mr. Benson, and Joey was honest saying that he was going to stay with them for the foreseeable future. He was terrified of his son. Rightly so, he told them.

"He can stay forever if he wishes." Yasmine laughed a little. "It'll be like having a grandda around, one that I never knew. Ed is a very nice man, and the dog is wonderfully polite."

It was settled then. Ed would stay here until

such a time he was in a better place. Or if he wanted until he was pushing up daisies, as the man had said of himself. Thinking this was the best move for all involved, Joey was glad to have the man close in the even that Junior, or whatever he was being called, came around.

~*~

Yasmine was nervous. She and Joey had been flirting all afternoon. Touching one another when passing. He'd kiss her on her neck, wrap his arms around her when he could. She was ready for him in the most desperate way. But she was also worried. Sex had been all right when she'd had it, but Yasmine had a feeling it wasn't going to be the same with Joey. It would be epic.

"You're shaking. Are you cold?" Yasmine told him she was nervous. "Nothing is going to happen unless you want it to. I'm serious when I say that. We have the rest of our lives to be together, and I don't want you to think I'm going to force you into anything."

"I don't. You're the sweetest man I know. Next to Ed, anyway." He tickled her, and she laughed with him. It served to break the ice too. "I love you, Joey.

So much I just don't know what to do with all of it."

"Loving me is the best thing in the world. I love you as well." He helped her take off her blouse. "You're way overdressed for the bedroom, love. You should be as naked as I am."

Leaning back into his chest, as he was behind her now, she could feel the soft hair on his chest. The muscles there too. When he wrapped his arms around her to her bra, she moaned when he lifted it up and cupped both her breasts at the same time.

"So lovely. I'm going to taste you all over." She moaned again. It was like he was adding gas to the fuel of sexual need for him. "Come with me."

He was forever gentle with her. He never made her feel like she was a burden to him. As he helped her strip off the rest of her clothing, he touched every inch of her as he revealed her skin. When she was naked, her body was wet with need.

"I can smell you. Christ. Your scent is calling to me. I need you."

He helped her to lie in the middle of the bed, and she felt her breath leave her body when he licked her navel, leaving her wetter than she'd been before.

Yasmine felt him get onto the bed with her. It

shifted her around with his weight. Once he stopped moving, he spread her legs so she could tell they were on either side of his hips. Running his hands up her legs and over her thighs, Yasmine held her breath for whatever he was going to do to her next.

When he licked her, swirling his tongue around her nether lips, she came hard. The breath she'd been holding escaped from her in a scream that felt like it was longer than any scream she'd heard.

"Oh, that was wonderful, love. I want it all."

Again he adjusted himself on the bed. Then he opened her neither lips and suckled at her clit hard and quick. Reaching down to touch him, Yasmine held onto him, her body not understanding if it wanted him to stop or keep at it.

It seemed like hours since he'd put her on the bed. Joey's hands and mouth had devastated her so many times that she was weak with it. Each time she came, Yasmine begged him to stop, but he continued to bring her over the edge of high peaks over and over.

When he stopped, his hands still holding her, Yasmine felt a dip in the bed again. He was making his way up her body. Kissing her hip. Nipping at her belly. At her breasts, he suckled them one at a time and both.

Arms weak, she couldn't move. Couldn't hold him any longer. As he made his way up to her neck, throat, and then ears, Yasmine felt a renewed strength roll over her. Like her body was ready for the rest, the best.

Joey kissed her then, allowing her to taste what he'd done to her. Wrapping her arms around his neck, she held him to her as his cock slipped deeply inside of her. The sheer length and width of it had her coming, made her scream out his name as he moved. When he took her over the edge like before, she knew that whatever happened now was going to make her love him all the more.

"Come for me, love. Come and let me fill you." Her body tightened up as if it was on a long pause. "Come."

The breaking of the pause had her feeling torn apart. Each stroke of his cock brought her closer and closer to the fall. And when she felt his cum, felt his own body stiffen as hers did, she held onto Joey so she'd not shatter, come apart, and leave him. Blackness took her under so quickly that she had no time to prepare for it.

Waking up, there was a chill in the room. Moving caused her to hurt a little, but she knew Joey was lying beside her. Aching just a little more, she moved so that she could lay her head on his chest. There is where she heard his heart beating.

"You broke me. I hope you know that." She laughed and kissed him where she'd had her head. "I have to honestly say that I've never in my life experienced anything even remotely close to that. How are you feeling?"

"Amazing. Wonderful. Sated. Sore too, but I still loved every second of that." Since she couldn't see, not sure she wanted to know, she asked him the time. "That late? My goodness. I must have really been out of it. Four in the morning is usually when I get up and do my best work."

Neither of them moved. As she laid there, dozing off and on, she listened to the house as it settled, like the sound of the air conditioner cooling off the room. Joey snored lightly, not really making much in the way of noise, and she let sleep take her under once again.

The next time she woke, Yasmine got out of

bed. It wasn't nearly as easy as she thought it should have been. Each time she got a little distance between her and Joey, he'd pull her back into his arms and snuggle.

Taking a shower helped with the sore muscles she had. Even her toes—she couldn't figure out why they were so sore—felt better for the shower. Dressing, using the system she'd thought of when she and Tabby had been out, she was confident in the fact that she had on matching clothing for the day.

Yasmine usually didn't wear anything but browns. But with Tabby's help, she was able to hand sew small braille tags on the hangers that told her what the piece of clothing looked like. Just simple things, like it was a plain blue shirt. Or even a yellow dress covered in daisies. That was what she was wearing today.

After having a very hardy breakfast, so happy that their cook was helpful in telling her where things were, she headed to the living room. Yasmine was going to have her things set up here so she could work.

Knowing she didn't have to work made her feel like she would enjoy her job more. Not that she didn't like what she was doing or make enough money, but she wasn't as pressured. Not having Jazzie around all the time helped too. Yasmine wondered what she was up to now.

The agent showed up about half an hour later. She and Joey had already picked out the room she was going to be using, so she showed him to the place. Joey had the list of things that were going to be needed put in, so the man set to work. Joey joined her while she was telling the agent that she needed him to set up the fax machine on the same secure network.

"I guess I never thought you'd need a fax machine. Or a printer." Yasmine explained to Joey how special her printer was. "I started to ask you if you were serious, but I know you are. I had no idea that — well, there are a great many things I'm learning about you. I bet that sucker isn't cheap either, is it?"

"I don't know. I mean, I have an idea that they're really pricy. Since they provide it for me at no charge, I didn't ask." She asked the agent if he knew what the price was. He told her. "My goodness. I wasn't even in the ballpark with ten to eighty-thousand dollars. I'm assuming this one is on the higher end."

"It is, ma'am. The highest. But it gets a very good rating, and I have set them up in a couple of schools for the blind. They love it too." Joey asked how they afforded that, what with it being so expensive. "Donations. They are always looking for help with their funding. My daughter teaches at the Mount Cherry School for the blind. She's not blind, but she said it's a lovely school. Their funding isn't as hard to come by as most places. The Anderson Foundation has kept them in supplies for a very long time."

"That's my brother. Before him, I'm sure, was his mom. I'll have to ask him if I can donate too." The agent thanked them again, and they left him to it. "I have to go out again. Sher is sick — a mild case of food poisoning, he told me. I guess he treated himself to a slice of pizza last night that was left over from his family's dinner, and he didn't realize it had set out all night. The sausage hadn't been cold."

"Poor man. I do hope he's all right." Joey told her he was doing better now that he was home with his wife taking care of him. "I can see him not allowing her to overwork herself. I'm betting if you were to go over there, she'd be sitting on the couch with her feet up, and he's sick in the kitchen making them a cup of tea."

They were both laughing as he left her. Going to the kitchen, she had herself a cup of tea and talked with the cook there. Mrs. Powder was a very nice woman and a great cook. She asked her if there was anything she couldn't or didn't eat.

"I'll try anything once. I'm not opposed to trying new dishes all the time. I do like a light lunch, so I'm not weighted down, and a little heavier dinner. Or supper in this area, I guess." She said she called it supper. "All right. As for what I can't eat, I can't have avocados. Not in any way or recipe. I break out in hives, and then I'm sick for several days afterwards. While I know you were talking food, I'm also allergic to tape. Any kind of sticky substance. It will tear my skin off and leave a welt there. If it's on too long, I get blisters. No Band-Aids. No paper tape either. If it's sticky, I can't have it on my body."

"That must be difficult if you have an emergency. I've been in the ER a few times, and they don't even ask you anything before they're shoving an IV in your arm and taping you up. And don't get me started on them electricity things. The thing that gives them a reading on your heart. Then when they're finished with you, they just leave them there on you." Mrs. Powder laughed a little. "One time I had me a pain in my chest so bad I hurt for it. Come to find out, they'd left one of them suckers there under my breast. Didn't think to check, but it sure did hurt when I washed there."

She spent an enjoyable couple of hours with the older woman. When the agent was finished with the inside work, it was Mrs. Powder who took him around to where the Internet came into the house. While they were outside, Yasmine went into her new office and felt the desk and where the computer was. She was so excited she couldn't wait to get started.

When her fingers touched a small container, she carefully picked it up. It was a planter, she realized, with a small succulent in it. Sure it was from Joey, she smiled. As she was putting it back on her desk, reminding herself to ask him when he got back, she heard the crunch of gravel in the driveway. Not knowing who it might be, Yasmine stayed where she was. There was no point in showing herself if she didn't have to.

Hearing Mrs. Powder talking in a calm voice to

whoever it was, Yasmine didn't let her guard down. It could be Jasmine, or the man that was related to Mr. Benson. The door shut soon after, and it wasn't until Mrs. Powder cleared her throat that she realized it wasn't trouble.

"There is a package for you, mistress. It's from an office in Washington. I was only told that." She said it was more than likely for her job. "Yes. I will put it here on the desk for you. If you'd not mind, I'd like for you to wait on Mr. Phillips. There is no telling the lengths that someone would go to."

"Yes, all right. That's a good idea." As soon as her cell rang, she answered it. Mrs. Powder must have left her when she answered the call, for she could no longer hear her breathing. It was the president. "Hello, sir. I was just getting set up here."

"Good. You've also received a package. I was notified as soon as it was scanned. Is Joey there with you?" She said he was on duty. "Good man. It's the cell phones we talked about. Yours is outfitted the way you wanted. It never would have occurred to me to have the letters in braille for someone. But there are a lot of them on the market nowadays. Also in the box are some gift cards. It's a wedding gift from me to the two of you."

"Thank you, sir. You didn't have to do that."
He said he'd enjoyed it. "I'll have Joey put them in his
wallet so the next time we're out, we can use them."

They talked about the work she was going
to be doing and how the networks would be ready
today. The agent that had come to the house to do it
was finishing up just as she ended the call with the
president. Everything was set up, and she was ready
to go. Yasmine had a lot of work to finish up.

Chapter 6

Jazzie was about as pissed as she'd ever been. Even more pissed off than she was at her sister right now, without even counting having to wait in this line to withdraw some cash for herself. Since she'd been here, nothing had gone right at all. And Yazzie was being about as stupid as she had been at any time of her life. But right now, it was costing Jazzie money.

The crew she had recruited for the bank job that should have happened several weeks ago was going to leave town if they didn't have some walking around money. Her gun had been taken from her by the police, or she would have just gotten rid of them and found herself another bunch of idiots to replace them. They were hobos until she'd found them, and now they needed cash, or they'd go to the police. Mother fuckers.

Taking another step up, the sixth person from her moved to a teller. Christ, this was going to take forever. Her not being able to demand that she get to the front of the line because she didn't have any gossip to impart was making her head hurt. What the hell could someone talk about for ten minutes after they got their banking done? Nothing, that's what. This was one of the million and one reasons she hated small towns.

Yazzie was going to pay her back for this. That was another thing that was making her broke—her sister wasn't paying her like she had before. Of course, she wasn't caring for her, not that she ever really did, but that wasn't the point. The point was that she could have been had Yazzie been where she wanted her to be. Which was in her little apartment that Jazzie had decorated herself. Good lord, it was loud with bright colors and eclectic in the furniture.

The scam of making sure the cameras saw her dressed up and looking like her crippled sister had been brilliant. Usually, she only had to give her a little dope to have her out like a stone, but this last time, she'd woken up. Way too soon for her to have gotten a single thing done that she'd wanted. Damn that woman. Taking another step forward, she only had five more people to go before she could take her money out.

Yazzie had been beaten badly because of her stupidity too. Jazzie had done it. She felt like her sister deserved it for what she'd done to her. Jazzie thought it was funny that her sister was still trying to figure out how that had come about. Because Jazzie had hit her a few times while Yazzie was sliding off the chair to the floor, her sister had broken her favorite China set. However, she didn't think it had been that bad. Of course, when she was in a rage, Jazzie rarely remembered what she'd been doing.

This time she was able to take two steps forward. Another teller, thank goodness, had opened up another workstation. She was just getting ready to pull out her checkbook when she heard a very familiar sound behind her—the racking of a bullet into the chamber of a handgun. Mother fuck, the place was going to be robbed.

The gunfire spread all over the ceiling of the

bank, raining down a lot of shit that she was sure would cause cancer. When ordered to get on the floor, she complied—they did both have guns, after all. But she didn't lay her head down as the man told her to. He put the gun to the back of her head and ordered her again.

"I will not. This floor is filthy. You have no idea how many feet have been stepping on this just today. Why, for all I know, it could have dog shit on it. No, not going to happen." He asked her if she would rather have dog shit on her face while breathing or when she was dead. "You're not going to kill anyone. Christ, if you were, you should have started with the guard over there. That's the way I'd do it."

"You'd do it? What are you, some kind of bank robber?" She didn't answer him. There were too many people around for her to confess to anything. "If you're so smart, bitch. What would you have done by now?"

"You've been fucking around with me so much that I'm sure one of the tellers has already pushed the silent call button to the cops." She saw the man turn to look at the stations. "Then there is the bank manager that is right now calling them to tell them there are two gunmen in the bank that are armed, and one of them is holding a gun to one of the customers' heads. You're a dumbass, you know that, don't you?"

Nodding to the other man, he went to where she assumed the bank manager's office was. The sound of a single gunshot told her that not only was this an armed robbery, but also murder. These men were dumber than she could have thought.

"Did you even think this through when you came in here? Did you even lock the door when you decided to shoot the place up?" Again she watched him nod to his partner, and the door was locked. "Have him look to see if the police have arrived yet while he's there."

"You're not in charge, bitch. Christ, I might just shoot you to shut you the fuck up." She told him she was being helpful. "Yeah? But you don't have to be a cunt about it too."

Rolling her eyes, she waited for the other man to confirm that the police were indeed out there. A lot of them. This was a small town, so she doubted very much there were more than two cops out there.

"Rollin, there are men out there with FBI on their jackets." Rollin popped the other man in the nose for saying his name. "Like it matters now. They're going to kill us both, and there ain't no coming back from that. Who the hell called the feds? You think they came here for us? Hey, that's great, right? That sure is going to be a big feather in our hats, don't you think? We'll be making a name for ourselves. We'll be dead as dead can be, but we'll be famous."

"Shut the fuck up."

She could tell that Rollin was getting nervous. She was too. While they'd been arguing, she noticed that one of the people on the floor was making a call. Pointing it out to him, she grinned when he shot the man in the head, blowing blood and gore all over the people around him. Then the screaming began.

It was a sound she usually liked to hear when she was robbing banks. It was no less exciting than when she was in charge, but she didn't think these men were enjoying it overly much.

Rollin walked over to the woman in the middle of the screamers and shot her. The way this was ending up, she might well be the only one that survived this shit. Jazzie knew that they'd ask her for advice soon, and she was going to make sure she got out of here with at least some cash in her pockets.

Sitting up so that she could see more of the room, she wasn't the least bit surprised when they ignored her. There were, so far, four dead, including the guard at the door, and there were fifteen or so people left in the room. Counting up the number of years they'd get if they survived, she figured they might be better off being killed by the cops.

"How come the drawers are all locked up?" Rollin asked the other man what he was talking about. "The cash out drawers. They're all locked up. What are we going to do now?"

Rollin asked her what was going on.

"The alarm was pressed. That makes the bank close up tighter than a nun's thighs in a room full of men." He asked about the vault. "You killed the only person that knows how to get into it. See, you need to have a better plan when you rob a bank. But I'm not going to be giving you free advice. When you talk to the police about what your demands are, I want a cut of that too."

"You think we're going to get out of here alive?" She shook her head. "Why the fuck not? We got hostages. Even if one of them is a pain in the ass."

"Just like your partner said, there are feds out

there, and they'll be just pissy enough about all the deaths in here for them not to be very accommodating in letting you get out of here with much." Rollin asked her why she was so smart. "I don't know, Rollin, perhaps because I pay attention and have a solid plan when I do something. You even scope out this place before you came in here shooting the place up and killing people? More than likely not."

"Then we should just kill everyone in here." The phone rang that was in the office, somewhere in the area where the other man had killed the bank manager. "What the hell is someone calling him now for? Don't they figure he's dead?"

"I'm assuming it's for you two." She waited while Rollin sent the other man to the office. When he handed the phone to her, she was going to tell whoever was on the other end what was going on, adding just enough fear and terror to her voice to make sure they hadn't any idea she was helping them. "This is Jazzie Dennis. We're being held hostage by some very bad men."

"Hello, Jazzie, it's Joey Phillips. Don't you think it's ironic to be a person in a bank robbery that you're not in charge of? I do. I've been laughing my ass off since I saw you in there." She felt her anger surge up so much that it seemed to close off her throat. "How many people have they killed? And I want you to know that I believe you're in on this. This is what you do for a living, isn't it?"

"I don't know what you're talking about. How the hell did you know I was in here?" He told her there were cameras all over the bank. "Christ, I would have cut that out before arriving."

His laughter had her realizing she'd given herself away. "Yes, I'm sure you would have done a great many things differently. However, I want you to tell the Dobbin brothers what I say to you. Do you think you can handle that?"

"I loathe you, Joey." He laughed again, and again her temper flared. "Why aren't you rushing in here to save these people? You have the feds out there, don't you?"

"We do, as a matter of fact. You'd be surprised to know that they're willing to allow Rollin or Ben to murder you, so your reign of terror is done too. I actually like that idea a great deal. You'd be out of our hair. Your sister will be happier, and— Did I mention that she no longer considers you her sister?

I forgot about that until just this second. You really pissed her off, didn't you?" She told him she wasn't going to be killed. That she'd struck up a deal. "Sure you have. How many more people do you think will die before you're just as dead as the others?"

"What do you want me to say to these men?" He told her, and she nearly gagged on the words she had to repeat. Jazzie knew they weren't telling the truth on this. "They said that if you let all the hostages out, they'll allow you to come out without killing you."

"What if I just kill them all?" She knew that Joey could hear them, so she waited for his reply. "Tell him we want a five million dollars and getting out of here free and clear. Also, tell him we're not going to do this again."

This time she repeated what Rollin had said to her.

"No, that's not going to work for us. They're not going to be leaving there under any conditions other than the ones I've stated or a body bag. It's entirely up to them. They'll be dead before they can get out the door if they don't comply." Jazzie told Joey he was being unreasonable. "Am I? So far, they've killed a lot of innocent people for nothing. The vault is locked, and so are the cash drawers. If they rob the people in there, they're more than likely only going to get a couple of hundred dollars. Tell them, Jazzie, before I start shooting."

She told the two men. There were several people crying quietly while Ben and Rollin thought about their options. Ben slid down to the floor in front of the bank of teller windows, and Rollin sat with him.

"We're fucked. You know that, don't you?" Ben nodded. "All right then. I have a better option. I love you, Ben."

The shot to his brother's head had her jumping. Rollin then turned the gun to his own temple and stared at her. Before she could say anything to Joey about the turn of events, Rollin pointed the gun at her and fired.

~*~

Yasmine didn't know what to feel. A part of her, a very small part, was saddened by her sister's death. But the relief of her not being around threatening her anymore was so much stronger. Her feelings on a great many things of late were messing with her mind.

"Are you all right?" She smiled at Tabby's question and told her she was just thinking. "Good. Thinking is better than regretting. She was a terrible person, Yasmine. Joey did tell you that she was helping the bank robbers throughout the entire thing, right?"

"Yes. She was responsible for the murder of three of the people. That poor guard had a new wife. And there isn't going to be much in the way of justice for them. They're all three dead." After Rollin had shot his brother then turned the gun on Jazzie, he'd killed himself. Such a waste of human life. "I wanted to thank you for suggesting that we donate her body to the Body Farm. I had no idea there was such a thing as that."

There was one such farm in Columbiana County, Ohio. That was where she'd sent Jazzie's body. It was a place where donated bodies were staged in different circumstances to watch them decompose. Sometimes they would tie the body to a tree to watch how long it took it to fall over. To see what sort of things happened to the extremities as they hung here. These things were used in determining the time and circumstances of a death. It was primarily used in solving murders, as well as suspicious deaths. Shivering a little, she smiled.

"When will the men be back? I'm guessing that this guy…what's his name again?" Tabby told her. "Martin Hamilton isn't aware that they're going to bring him back here. I'm to understand he's had a very difficult life too."

"All of them have but Caleb. Harlin Bentley has just lost his job because of cutbacks. They're still having some difficulty chasing down Daniel Watson. The last known address for him turned out to be a vacant lot. After running that down, they were able to figure out that he did indeed live in the apartments that had been there, but the city decided that tossing them out and razing everything was a good solution. Sometimes I think cities should be run by the people actually doing the living in towns. You know, put someone that is homeless in charge of seeing that the homeless are taken care of. I'm not sure how or if that would work, but they'd have a damned sight better view than someone that has a million-dollar home would." Yasmine laughed. "Yes, well, I do get on my soapbox on occasion."

"You do at that. When is Melissa going to be here? I'm about to starve." Tabby said she'd give her a call. "No, don't do that. I'm sure she'll be here soon. I might have to get myself a cookie or something to tide me over."

Almost as if Melissa had heard them, she was pulling into the drive. She really liked the elderly woman. Sheppard as well. They were kind, loving, and full of life now that they were in Caleb's life.

"Oh my, I'm running behind. But it's Sheppard's fault entirely. He wanted to go with us to lunch, and then he didn't. I swear, that man drives me nuts. I'm so glad Caleb took him with them this morning." Tabby asked how he'd made her late if he was gone. "The things I laid out for me to wear today; the man had actually put them away. I can't get him to put his socks in the hamper right there in the bathroom, but he can put my clothing away when I don't want him to. He even stuck my shoes, the ones I couldn't find, in someplace that I'm going to brain him over when he returns."

They were all three still enjoying the antics of the Anderson household as they got into the car. Melissa kept them laughing all the way to the restaurant.

They were seated immediately, and Tabby put some veggies on a plate in front of her. Taking the carrots, she moaned at the sweet, crisp taste.

"I skipped breakfast in honor of this meal. I've heard that they have the best cod in the world. I love any kind of fish. Grilled tuna steaks are my favorite." Melissa told them that she'd eaten mahi-mahi once and hadn't cared for it. "You'll have to come over sometime when we're having a feast. I think Joey loves it more than I do. Last week we had so much food we couldn't eat it all."

They agreed that they'd enjoy having dinner at their home. After their orders were taken, they got down to business. This was a charity meeting, and they were going to set things up for whatever charity needed them the most. Yasmine wasn't sure what she'd be able to help with, but she was willing to pitch in however they needed her.

It took them nearly five hours to get things organized. Even though the restaurant was busy, they were never asked to leave. Yasmine supposed that was because they knew Caleb and Tabby had a great deal of money. Laughing to herself, Yasmine told herself to behave.

Exhausted from sitting for so long, they decided to walk around the open-air mall for a while. There were so many things to enjoy. The scents of the spice market. The grinding of the coffee mill. She even enjoyed the banter between customers and shop owners.

After getting help with a few purchases, they were ready to call it a day. She'd heard from Joey twice. Apparently, Martin was super stubborn and didn't think they were being serious. The second time he called her was to tell her that they were on their way home. Home. That word was becoming her favorite word. And feeling.

"I'm not sure what your plans are for Thanksgiving, which I know is a few months away, but I'd like to host some kind of get together for the family. This will be our first one with Caleb, as well as Christmas, and I want to have you all over too. I think of all of you as my grandchildren." Tabby and she thanked Melissa. "Christmas is going to be such fun, I think. Again, our first with our new family."

"Have you seen my dad, Jimmy?" Yasmine put her hand over Tabby's since she was close enough to her after hearing the question put to someone in one of the outdoor stalls. "He's got people all over my property out by the big barn. I was wondering where he's gotten to. He's not at home. That's for sure."

"No. I mean, I've seen him around town a few times. Let me think on when that was." The man paused. Yasmine asked Tabby if it was Junior Benson. At her telling her that it was, she asked her to call the police. "You know, now that I think on it, it's been a few days. Haven't seen the dog either, for that matter. Sometimes, you know, he lets her run, but not in the last few days, I don't think."

Tabby moved them a little further away from where they'd been standing. Yasmine could still hear the two men talking, but she wasn't near them. Their voices had faded as the two of them had speculated on where Mr. Benson had gone. She also heard Tabby talking to the police.

Holding onto the arm offered, she knew it was Melissa. "Come on, child. Let's get out of the way of the trouble brewing. I believe he's asking everyone in the stalls here if they've seen his dad. Do you know where he is?" Yasmine told her he'd gone with the men. "Well, that'll be a safe place for him to be. You said they were on their way back, correct? Maybe

Joey can come out here and see what is what. I know he's been helping the police a good bit."

"He has been." She wondered then if anyone had told their husbands and asked Melissa to do so now. Instead, she handed her phone to her, and Yasmine asked who she was speaking to. It was Joey. "Junior is here in the outdoor malls. Asking after his dad."

"Ed is at the police station with Caleb." She asked him where he was. "Setting up. Stay where you are, love. I don't want you hurt too."

Yasmine knew what that meant. He was lining up a shot to take the man out with as little involvement as possible. She had a feeling they were doing it this way so the police didn't have more deaths on their hands while taking out a man that had killed eleven people that they'd found out on the land.

Putting the phone away when Joey told her he needed to go, she asked Melissa and Tabby to go with her. That she needed to get as far as possible from Junior. Hearing the screams of the people behind her, she knew Joey had come through for the department again. She was so very proud of the man she could have jumped for joy.

She and the other women were headed home when she heard from Joey again. Asking him how he was doing, he told her that he was only going to be all right with what he'd done if she was. Yasmine asked him what he meant.

"I just killed a man. Shot him in the back of the head, and he dropped to the ground. Are you all right with that?" She asked him if he'd done it out of malice or even for fun. "No. I'd never do that."

"Did you do it because he was a good man that you decided didn't need to live any longer? Let me answer that one. No, you did what was required to get a monster off the planet. Will it haunt you? I hope not. What you did was very brave and very good." He thanked her. "No, it's me that thanks you. I was forever worried about Ed when he left the house. I think he's been staying indoors a little too much lately, but I think he was just as afraid as we were for him." Joey told her that he loved her. "And I love you. I'm headed home with the rest of the women. I'll see you when you're finished up. I'm sure you have a lot of paperwork to finish filling out."

"I do. And since the Feds asked me to do this, they need things to be perfect."

After telling him again that she loved him, Yasmine felt a great deal better. All in a day's work, she thought to herself.

As soon as he was home, she peppered him about the new brother. Since he was staying at Caleb's for a few nights, just to recuperate, she asked him about that as well. Why he was in need of medical care too.

"As you know, his name is Martin. He looks so much like Caleb that there is no way to think they're anything but brothers. Martin is, or was, a stockbroker. But he had an anxiety attack one day and hasn't been able to return to work. Not surprisingly. I've known a couple of stockbrokers that were living under a bridge with me. It's an extremely competitive job, as well as highly stressful." She asked him if he was going to be all right. "Yes. He's following his doctors' orders. When we stopped to get something to eat on the way home, he stuck to his diet. Martin told us he had had a terrible scare with what had happened, and he wasn't going to get to that point again. I can imagine that would scare the shit out of a person."

"I've had a couple of anxiety attacks myself,

but nothing just taking a few deep breaths in couldn't help." Joey kissed her on the nose. "Tell me all about him. Please? I need something to occupy my mind, or I'm going to go up to bed without anything to eat. You have to admit, it's been a very long few days."

"Tell me about it." He stretched out on the couch; she could feel by the way the cushions moved that he'd done it. "Let me see. He's a year older than Caleb and a year younger than me. His wife died some time ago from a car accident. She was hit by a drunk driver that walked away. Martin has some money. Not like Caleb does, but enough that he's putting his house on the market in a couple of days and could well afford to pay for a second house while waiting for the sale to go through. He has dark hair like we all do. Tall, again like Caleb and myself. As for believing we're all related, I'm not sure he believes that yet. His mom died just after he got into high school. If he said what had killed her, I didn't hear. No children. He has one sister and two brothers by his stepfather. Also, like us, he knew he was fathered by Howard Berkley. I'm not sure if he is aware of the way he might have been conceived, but he does know about Berkley."

"It's so sad, don't you think, that for as much effort as Abby put into finding these men, she doesn't get to meet them. I wonder what she would have said to them. More than likely welcomed them in much the same way Caleb has." Joey told her how they had hugged when they met him at his house. "Did that go over well? I mean, to get a hug is nice, but with men the size of you and Caleb, it must have been slightly overwhelming."

"It was." Joey laughed. "I think he was afraid to hug him back at first. You know Caleb, he can be like a big teddy bear most of the time. Well, he was a little teary eyed when Martin pulled away from him. I can only imagine what was going through his mind while he was getting crushed by his half-brother." She asked him if he'd hugged the other man. "I'm not sure, but I had a feeling that had I tried, it wouldn't have gone over well. He wasn't standoffish, but he was a little afraid, I think. I know I was slightly afraid when I first met them. But then I was sitting there where they found me with a gun in my hand."

"Tabby told me. I think she was worried you might try that again. I hope not, Joey. I would join you if something were to happen to you." They didn't speak for a few minutes. When the phone rang in the offices, she was almost ready to tell the caller to fuck off. But when Joey came back to her, she could almost feel his energy. "Good or bad? To be honest with you, Joey, I don't know that I can take too much more bad shit coming around."

"They've found your niece. She's only three hours from here. Would you like to go and get her?"

She was up and ready to go in just a few minutes. Both excited and nervous, she kept herself in line by repeating what she was doing until she was finished with the task.

"Putting on my shoes. Putting on my shoes."

Then when she was walking to the car, she did the same. Oh, to see this little girl one time would be so wonderful. But she'd have to be happy to find out what was happening in her life.

Chapter 7

Joey watched the little girl closely. She had that look of a person who had seen it all and wasn't the least bit impressed with anything around her. If she stayed in the system for much longer, he could almost see the real damage that would have been done to her, both physically and mentally. As it was, she was sporting a bruised lip and three stitches in her cheek.

"Nobody wants me." Yasmine told Madison that they did. "Until the money comes in and the people get too busy to come around anymore to be impressed on what you did. Then what will you do to me? I'm not a slave for you to use up."

"Calm the fuck down, kid. No one is going

to make you into a slave." She eyed him. That was when Joey noticed her eyes. They were so blue they were clear. Getting down on his knees as Yasmine had done, he put his finger under her chin to lift her face up. He was surprised when she allowed him to do that. "Was this an accident, or did someone slap you around?"

She jerked from him, but he did see the look she had on her face just as she did. Fear, and a quick glance around to the people there with them. He had a feeling that they'd done it and had told her to keep her mouth shut. Standing up, he reached for Madison's hand. Again, he was shocked that she let him.

"Did one of you assholes hit my daughter? Which one of you did it so that I can wipe the floor up with your blood?" Yasmine stood up too and fumbled out for Madison's hand until the little girl took it. "I'm still waiting on an answer."

"Is that what she told you? That we beat her? We're allowed to discipline them when they get mouthy and don't do their work. Everyone here has a job to do. But whatever. You do know that if you take her and bring her back, she'll be considered unadoptable and won't be around for people to pick again." He asked the woman in charge of the place what she meant by saying she wasn't going to be around. "Nothing. Just that she'll be put in her room and —"

"They lock me in my room. Today was the first time in forever that I was able to have a bath." Yasmine asked Madison to come with her, and they'd wait for Joey outside. "No. They're sneaky and get you when you're not looking. I have to watch his back. He's the first person that hasn't hit me when he touched me. I won't let them hurt him either."

Joey heard Yasmine talking to Madison. As soon as their voices began to fade behind him, he looked at the three people in front of him when one of them snickered. He asked them what was so funny.

"You, if you think you're going to be taking her out of here today. If ever. She's been a good little worker here, and we really don't want her to get away. For a little brat, she's handy to have around." Joey felt his temper get the better of him and had to take in several breaths before he trusted himself to speak. However, the man in the middle of the two men and one woman spoke again. "You'll learn that you have to slap them around a little bit before you can get them to see things your way. Like that one. She's a smart kid like I said, but she also has a big mouth."

"You've been using her as your housemaid while the other kids get to go off and play. Or is that staged too?" The three of them laughed. "All right. What did you mean by saying I wasn't going to take her out of here?"

"You can take her into the yard, but you'll never get past our security. And one call to the police, and she'll be right back here where she belongs, and you and your wife will be in jail. Kidnapping holds a dear fine, I heard." He said nothing to any of them as Middleman continued. "The woman who brought her and her brother here made it quite clear that we could do whatever we wanted with the children. And that if we played our cards right, she'd be bringing us a lot more children to do the same with."

"Jasmine Dennis." They looked a little shocked that he knew who their benefactor was, but they recovered nicely. Joey was still trying to figure out if there was a brother and sister that had belonged to Jasmine or did the man just mean there was a boy and a girl here. "If she was sending you money or anything, I'm afraid that bank has dried up. She was killed the other day during a robbery. So I guess it will suck for you three when it comes to more children."

The three of them put their heads together. Joey wished that Yasmine was here so she could tell him what they were saying. When his cell phone rang, and he saw Caleb's face, he decided to answer.

"I'm a tad busy right now, Caleb. Can I call you back?" Caleb told him that Yasmine had called him. "Yes, well, she doesn't know the half of the shit going on here. I'll have to call you —"

"I just bought the building. And the land surrounding it as well. I'm going to have the place torn down to the ground. So the idiots that you're speaking to will be out of a job. Not that it matters. They're going to be arrested soon enough." The three in question turned toward him. "Just hold the fort down for a few more minutes, little brother, and you're going to have more help than you know what to do with. See you when you come home."

Putting his phone away, he made a show of letting them see his holster and gun. The woman on the right started yelling about no guns being in the place, but he ignored her. He had to remain calm, and he was going to do that even if it caused his hair to turn white.

"I'm an agent for the FBI. I'm also a federal marshal. Those are my new titles I got the other day when I had to snipe a person for them. I'm an officer too, of the Dresden branch of the police department in my hometown." He showed them his new shiny badge, along with his identification. The door behind him exploded inward, and he was just barely able to get out of the way before about a dozen men and women in gear came in with their guns at the ready. "And these people are here to arrest the lot of you."

It was another hour before he was able to go and check on Yasmine and Madison. It had taken him that long to locate the little boy that belonged to Jasmine after finding the paperwork that was locked away in the office. Christ, she'd not even changed their name so that they couldn't be traced back to her. For which he was grateful. The other children, only five total counting Madison and her brother, had been locked in their rooms. The children that had been playing in the yard when they arrived were just school-aged children that had shown up to play on the equipment.

He'd had to carry Michael out of the place, as he'd been tied up for so long that there were burn marks on his legs. Christ, he was glad he hadn't known that before the police arrived, or he might well have said fuck it and killed the three people that were supposed to be in charge. As soon as Michael saw Madison, he wanted to go to her. Joey sat him down on the step and held Madison's hand.

"There is a little boy in front of you, Yasmine. He's your nephew. His name is Michael Dennis, and he's eight years old." Yasmine put out her hands to allow the boy to come to her. Joey looked at Michael before speaking. "Remember what I told you about my wife? How she can't see but uses her hands to touch people so she can sort of see you? Well, if you'd allow her to touch you, I'm sure she'll be as careful as she can be about your wounds. All right?"

"Yes, sir. But me and my sister, you said we'd go home with you and not have to be here again. Since I'm hurt, you can just take Maddy. I would rather her get safe than the two of us if it comes to that." Joey told him he was coming too. "Well, sir, we won't give you a lick of trouble. I promise you."

"I hope you do. Give us trouble, I mean. I want you to run through our yard at home and scream out your delight. To get dirty and need your knees and elbows bandaged up. I might not hit the sore place right at first, but I will be there for hugs when you need them. We have the nicest man living with us too. Ed. He'll be so happy to have you around. Then there are the Andersons. My goodness, I just realized how many relatives you're going to already have." Joey watched as Michael moved toward Yasmine slowly. She spoke again when she could touch her fingers to his cheek. "If I could see right now, I'd go in there and beat those people until they knew what it was like for someone to hurt you. To hurt a child is just wrong on so many levels. Had I known about you sooner, I would have moved heaven and earth to come for you both."

Since they had to stay in town until things were settled with the home, they decided to get something for dinner. However, they made a stop at the emergency room first. Michael said he was hurting too badly to be sitting up, and one look at his bottom, where he said they hit him, had them taking him there. Madison was checked over as well.

The doctor came to see him in the room Michael and Maddy were sharing. Both were exhausted and finally sleeping soundly.

"Madison has a few fresh bumps on her head. We'll get an X-ray in the morning for that. I think they've been poked at enough for one night. She's malnourished and dehydrated—nothing a few good meals and a lot of loving won't cure." Yasmine asked about Michael. "Aside from the harsh beating he got—I'd say a whip was used on him—he too is malnourished and dehydrated. He has a couple of old breaks in his left ribs that I'm wondering about and two more on the other side. In addition to that, he's also been knocked around with what could only be described as boots. I've taken pictures of their wounds and filled out the form that the police will need. I've already called them and told them your little family is here."

"Thank you, Doctor. I don't know when they'll be able to be released from the police, but you give them the best of care while they're here, please. I didn't know they were around until recently." The doctor patted Yasmine on the shoulder and told her she'd be just fine. "I hope so. I want them to have a better life than they have had."

"They will. Caleb Anderson called here about an hour after you arrived. He said the same thing that I was to make sure these kids and the other three brought here had the very best." Joey asked him what was to happen to them. "I don't know, young man. I would imagine they'll either end up in the system, or they'll be put into another home. I can send a social worker here for you to talk to in the morning if you'd like to know."

"I would. We would." He didn't even have to look at Yasmine to know they might be taking all five of the children home with them. They were all in the same dire need of food and drink. But mostly, they needed someone to love them. To care for them. "Joey?"

"Yes, love." She asked him about the other children. "You mean our five kids? I'd say they're going to be just fine, don't you think?"

"We only came here for Madison. I'm thinking that having them all together might make them adjust a little better, don't you?" He said that was something he had no idea about. "Me either. But I would feel better at night if I knew they were all safe."

"I couldn't agree more." While the children slept, he told her what he could remember about the other three. "One more girl. I think her name is Carol. I think I was told that she's six. The other two are boys, Shawn age five, George age three. None of the others are related. However, they're very close to each other."

"Good. I just want them to be in a safe environment so that I can love them to pieces." Yasmine got up to stretch then sat back down. She looked as exhausted as he was feeling right now. She would no more leave this room than he would. Joey wondered aloud if they could bring the other three in here. "I'll check on that."

Joey was still laughing when a nurse came back with Yasmine to say they'd have to have smaller beds, but it would be just fine. Taking out the extra chairs, in less time than he thought it would have taken him to figure things out, there were five children in the room with him and Yasmine.

Michael woke up for a few moments when they were shuffling things around. He just looked around for his sister, then laid back down, reaching for her hand. Joey had a moment of panic when Michael said he was hungry. But he went back to sleep before telling him what he wanted. The doctor had asked that they have no food until tomorrow's test.

Taking a trip down the hall, he realized that he had a lot of house to prepare. Not only that, but he didn't know the first thing about buying whatever supplies the kids were going to need. Clothing was the least of his problems, he thought when it came to getting them all ready at the same time to go someplace. Joey did the only thing he could think of and called Sher Kimble.

"You did what? Five at one time? Christ man, I was nearly in over my head with just one." Joey told him what had happened. "Then I'm very proud to call you my friend for that. No, no child should have to be put into one of those places. Much less one that is poorly run. What can I do for you?"

"I don't know what they'll need. I know clothing, toothbrushes, and stuff like that. But what kind of clothing? Do they need me to fit them for shoes? What will they eat?" Joey didn't appreciate the man laughing at him and told him that. It didn't help, Sher kept laughing. "I have five little kids that are going to be naked with dirty teeth if you don't stop laughing."

"I'll help you. I'll help. I really needed that laugh. Thank you. All right, Joey, I'm going to call my mom, and she'll gather up what you need. Tabby too." Joey said to get them whatever they'd need. "You might want to temper that before they become teenagers. They'll hold you to that if you don't. But I'll take care that they're outfitted for the first few days. Then you can take them shopping. Does anyone know but me?"

"I should have called Caleb first. I hope he's not pissed off." He asked him why he thought he would be. "I don't know, Sher. Because I have five kids that I didn't start with this morning. I'm going to need a second job after this."

After disconnecting the call, he made his way back to the room. Yasmine was sleeping in the lounger that had been brought in for them, with Carol sleeping in her arms. He couldn't have asked for a better partner in life than this woman right here.

After settling into his own chair, he pulled the blanket up and over him. He was a dad. That thought scared the shit out of him more than a little. Then he remembered the look on Maddy's face when she asked him if he was going to keep her. Telling her that she was his daughter was the best feeling he'd ever had since falling in love with Yasmine.

~*~

"I'm not sure why I wonder this, but is there anything left in the stores after you guys left there?" Tabby laughed with Yasmine. "I can feel six bags on this bed, and I'm sure you were only supposed to get the essentials. Joey said something about dirty teeth and being naked."

"It was hard for us to know the sizes. Mrs. Kimble said we should get an array of sizes to fit them. She also had us get things that would be for a much younger child. They are tiny little things, aren't they, Yasmine?" Yasmine told her what the doctor had told them. "They look good, don't get me wrong there. But they're very tiny."

"We'll get them healthy and ready to face a new world soon enough." Tabby envied the other woman and told her so. "I don't want to say anything around the kids, but I have never been so terrified as I am right now. Five little people are going to be depending on me, and I haven't any idea what I'm doing. I guess I don't have to worry about setting them down and losing them. I'm sure they'll find me."

"Yes, well, good riddance to your sister. Have you told the children she's gone?" Yasmine told her that Joey had told them both. "Did they act like they knew her? Or even recognized who she might have been to them?"

"They knew the name but nothing more. The people that were running that monster house were getting paid each month from a fund that had been set up. The banker said he'd make sure it was sent to us from now on. It's a fund that feeds itself. I'm not sure what that means. Caleb and Joey got together with an attorney to see about my sister's money and her house. To see if any of it could go for the kids." Tabby asked about the other three. "They'll all get a fifth of it. Whatever amount it comes to be, it'll never be enough to make up for what she did to them. I blame my sister for all five of them being put in that place and ill-used."

The two of them tagged the clothing for the children. Not for the kids to know what they were wearing, but so Yasmine felt more comfortable. A side effect was that Maddy and Mikey, as they had been calling him, would be able to learn braille too, as they had said they wanted.

Tabby loved the little girly outfits that had been purchased for the girls. There were also shorts and T-shirts for them to play in. However, seeing little Carol with her hair pulled up in ponytails and her shiny shoes, she called them, melted all their hearts. Maddy was adorable too, but she was still adjusting to having things, so she didn't act as if she was impressed. Tabby hoped the little girl could keep that trait. Not looking impressed at times would save her a lot of heartache, she thought.

"Yasmine, can you show me how to read?" Tabby wasn't sure what to say—there wasn't any way she could help little Carol. "I don't mean words like the ones that people use. But the special ones you use."

Looking at her friend, she could see she was having difficulty in speaking for a moment. Tabby took Carol over to her new clothing and showed her the braille tabs that were on their clothing. After explaining to her that the words were there as well, Carol seemed about as excited as she'd been with her original question.

The kids had been out in the yard with Ed for most of the morning. When lunchtime rolled around, he wheeled in Mikey to the table and made them pizza rolls, a treat for all of them. Tabby stole one off the kids' plates to hear them laugh, but it was Yasmine that got the biggest laughter from them.

"So, are you eating a giant slice of pizza rolled into a tiny tube? Does it explode in your mouth once you bite into it?" Carol handed her one. They watched as she tentatively bit into it and then laughed when Yasmine made her cheeks full of air. "These are good. I've actually never had one before, but I can see the appeal of them. What would you guys like to have for dinner tonight? I'm not cooking so that it will be good. We can grill out, go out, or just have something comforting to eat."

While the kids asked questions of the different options for dinner, it occurred to Tabby what a natural Yasmine was at being their mom. She didn't talk down to them. Nor did she make them feel like their question didn't deserve an answer. Yasmine treated them like they were her children and that she loved them already. Tabby thought the kids were falling in love with Joey and Yasmine too. Even little George, who was about as adorable as a kid could be, seemed to be in love with his new momma.

Tabby held George as the other kids went into the backyard again. Ed had had a swing set put in the back for the kids, and they were "helping" the builders put it together. The men were good natured about their being underfoot, and Tabby wondered if he'd paid them a little extra to let this go on. Whatever the reason was, they were all enjoying themselves.

Shawn crawled up into Joey's lap a few minutes after he and Caleb had come back. He, like George, was asleep a few minutes after getting settled. Tabby realized then that Joey was going to be the best father to the children. And he and Yasmine together were going to be so happy.

The two men had been out with Martin, letting him look over the houses. However, he wasn't ready to move just yet, he told them. The man was so tense it worried her somewhat. Caleb told her that he was here but sitting in the living room until he could feel comfortable with them. Too many people, he'd told her.

"I'd think this was the wrong house to bring

him to, Caleb. There are five little ones here that are too excited to be calm around him." He told her that was where he wanted to go. "Well, perhaps this will be trial by fire for him. There isn't any way he'll be able to keep the kids from peppering him with a thousand questions."

"I hope they do." She could see the merit in that as well. But she didn't want to see the man go into the hospital again either. "He needs, as you said, to mingle with others. This way, he can simply walk away if he needs to. Go to another room to chill. But he knew the kids were here before he asked to come here. We're having dinner here with him and the others as well."

"The kids want to have a cookout. I don't know what all she ordered, but Yasmine has ordered all kinds of salad mixtures, along with steaks and brats with the hotdogs. Why don't they have a staff here?" Caleb told her he thought that now the kids were here, they'd hire some. "Yes, she's going to need all-hands-on-deck with this lot. But I do so love them all."

"I do too. All of them. That George, he's a cutie. However, I do worry about Shawn. He looks like he's calculating all the time. Not in a bad way, like where to stick the knife, but just looking for threats. I'm not making any sense, am I?" She told him she understood. "I just hope he can learn to relax somewhat. Always looking for danger is going to make him old before his time."

All the kids looked like they'd been through a great deal. Michael had the most physical wounds to his body, but he was also careful not to get too close to anyone. Male or female, he kept his distance until he trusted a person.

Carol was the most outspoken. She was only six, but Tabby had a feeling the little girl could fight off a man twice the size of Caleb and do some serious damage to him. She was particularly close to George, in a way that had her thinking the little girl had protected him a great deal while they'd been in the home.

Maddy was very unsure of herself, right up until she wasn't. Laughing a little as she watched the children playing on the slide, Tabby wondered what stories the six-year-old had to tell. She also wondered if Maddy being unsure of herself had anything to do with protecting herself from the adults at the home.

None of them had been sexually abused, but that didn't mean they weren't exposed to some from the people there.

Shawn was a typical five-year-old, she thought. A million and one questions that just about all started with "what if." Then there was the "why" question when he'd about exhausted any other questions he might have had. He and Maddy could have passed for twins in that they were both blue eyed and blond. There had been DNA tests done on all the children, and they'd have to wait and see if the little boy belonged to Jasmine too.

George was a charmer. He would get into your lap so long as you didn't help him. Tabby supposed all three-year-olds were like that, needing to show their independence. There were scars on his back, cigarette burns she thought they looked like, and she wondered who on earth could do something like that to a child. His favorite statement so far was, "I got it."

Yasmine had signed the kids up for school the day after they had arrived home. Also found them a doctor that they could go to, as well as a therapist. The list of things she was going to get taken care of looked like something that might have come from a book on how to raise children. However, it was written by someone that had actually raised them, not someone who had theories on how to do a good job. Not that she thought they didn't have good ideas as well, but she, like Yasmine, trusted someone who had actually done the deed more than someone that had only observed it being done.

The kids were getting tired, so they all went into the house. Dinner would be made soon, and they needed to get cleaned up. The kids didn't make a whiney sound at all about having to come in but were polite and came to Yasmine right away when she called for them. Tabby wanted to hang out around here when she had kids, so they could see the proper way to listen to parents. However, she didn't know if this would last very long here. They would be teenagers someday.

Chapter 8

Martin put his hands under his legs. Trying to maintain a distance wasn't going to work, he realized when the kids came and stood in front of him. He'd been just about ready to go out on the deck — a little at a time, his therapist told him — but they started coming in. The little girl, he didn't know their names, just then got up on the couch with him and leaned close and laid her head on his shoulder. Martin was ready to leap up and run when she spoke to the other children.

"You remember that kid that was jumpy all the time?" They nodded, though he doubted the youngest had any idea what she was talking about. "You remember that they had to take him away one night? On account'a him screaming all night?"

"Yeah, he wasn't right in the head." The little girl told the speaker to hush and to behave. "I didn't mean it in a bad way, Carol, but he was messed up in the head on account'a the drugs that his mom and dad gave him. Did someone give this man drugs?"

"No, they didn't. I'm not good around people." The little boy told him they were kids, not people. "Why would you think that makes any difference? I mean, you're still a person, right?"

"I guess so. But we won't ever hurt you none." Martin said he wasn't worried about them hurting him rather than the other way around. "You won't hurt us either, Mr. Hamilton. You're hurting in a place that needs to be fixed. Am I right?"

"Something like that. I was working one day and had a nervous breakdown. I couldn't take it any longer and decided to end my life." He'd not even told Caleb that when he'd asked him about his health. When the little girl pulled his hand out from under his leg, Martin let them see the scars there. She ran her little finger over the fresh scar, and Martin could feel some kind of kid magic coming from her. "I let my job nearly kill me. I should have paid attention to my mind and body, but I thought I was above all that. I thought it would just go away. But all it did was make me sicker and sicker."

The kids sat on the floor except for the little girl. Martin didn't know why he was able to talk to these children. He'd already told them more than he had anyone before. By degrees, he felt his body begin to relax, his mind clear of the need to take flight.

"My mom did that. Cut up herself in the bathtub one day while I was at school." Martin told the little boy he was sorry for his loss. "My name is Shawn. I was seeing a doctor after my mom died, and I found her lying there. Until my dad thought I was too much of a burden for him. He got himself a new wife, too, who didn't want me around. But my mom, she was good to me. Made me a nice cake for my birthday. My doctor told my dad I was way more depressed than he was and that I needed to keep seeing someone about it. These kids here, they helped me."

"My mom is gone too. Cancer." The kids all told him they were sorry. "Thank you for that. I'm wondering if that had a little to do with my breakdown."

"Yeah, everything does." The little girl next to him told him her name was Maddy. "Mine and Mikey's mom sold us off to the home we was at. Yasmine and Joey are going to adopt us all if there isn't anyone looking for the others. But Yasmine is my aunt on account'a her being our mom's sister. She's dead too, our mom, though I don't know nothing about her."

He'd known that too, of course, but hearing the accounting of it was…Martin didn't know, but he thought it was charming in a way. Less harsh than thinking about what he'd been told about Jasmine Dennis.

It wasn't long before they had him adjusting his seating, so he had two kids on either side of him. George was in his lap snoozing, and the other four were talking around him. Martin thought this was the best he'd felt in a good long time. Just them talking around him and not screaming and yelling at people.

He looked up when he heard someone whisper his name. It was Yasmine. Apparently, at some point, the kids had wandered off, and he'd been snoozing himself.

"Are you all right?" He told her he'd only just been thinking. "I've been feeling the same sort of special magic they can give off. Even George has his own type of magic."

He watched her move to the other couch. She sat in the middle, directly across from him. Laughing just a little, she smiled and asked him if she'd done something stupid again.

"I doubt anyone would think anything you did was stupid, Yasmine. You're much too beautiful for that. I was just admiring how you get around in the house. And when you sat across from me, I thought for sure that I'd been fibbed to about your blindness." She thanked him for not calling her a cripple or handicapped. "I'm assuming from what I heard about your sister, that's who called you that."

"Yes, it was her. A lot of other people too, but my sister knew better. I only told her several times a day." She didn't elaborate, so he didn't pry. "You seem really relaxed right now. So I don't want to tense you up by asking the wrong questions. I'm assuming you believe that you're related to my husband and Caleb now. What are your plans if you have thought them through?"

"I've not. Not really. I have a home back in Tennessee. There are a great many memories there. While here, believe it or not, I've realized that they weren't all good ones either. My mom was a great person, but she was bitter too. Not just for having to raise me without help, but about everything. She was unhappy a great deal of the time. But I loved her." Yasmine told him that, of course, he did. "Not that she made it easy for me. Mom showed me how to live on my own. How to deal with overdue collection calls and mail. Just trash them until it was going to be shut off or taken away. Food from the kitchen was hit or miss. Mostly the missing part. But she did love me too. And told me that every day."

"I plan to do that with the others too. Tell them how much I love them. How proud I am about something they've done. I've never been a mom before and have very little to go by as a role model. I'm going to wing it, as I've heard Ed say on occasion." He laughed, another thing he'd missed doing since he'd been stressed. "What is it you want to do with your life now that you're here? The world is open for you. I've only just discovered, now that there is no pressure on me to work, I enjoy my job a good deal more."

"I used to be a stockbroker. I never really liked it, not even at the beginning. It paid well, and I was good at it. If push came to shove, I'd rather live on the streets than to have to go back to something like that." He thought about her question and what she'd said about her own job. "I'd like something like that. Something I could do and just be able to enjoy. One of the things I used to do was grow plants. Just little things like tomatoes and lettuce. It supplemented our food at home, and I could spend hours out in the sunshine. I even got to where I was growing little things in the house."

"I have plants in my office. When I'm needing something to bring me out of my thoughts, I just need to reach over and touch them. Joey got me a couple of herbs too that I can smell. It's lovely. Why don't you do that for a living?" He asked her what she meant. "I'm fairly certain there is a need for a greenhouse around here. I know there used to be one. If I were to ask, I'm betting Caleb might even own the building."

"I don't know that I'm ready to embark on something like that." She stood up, and he did as well. "I didn't mean to offend you if I did."

"You didn't. I just need to see to dinner." She started for the doorway, again looking like a person with sight, and turned back to him at the last moment. "Four days ago, I didn't know I had a niece *and* a nephew. Four days ago, I didn't have any children to speak of. Four days ago, I made a decision that would change the course of my life and those of the five kids that I now have. I had no experience with children. I knew nothing of how to make sure they were fed well. Being blind didn't even come into the picture until we were all here. Was it a great deal? Hell yeah. Was I overwhelmed? Yes, right up until one of them took my hand into theirs. Would I do it again? Without hesitation. You should think more along the lines of how things will affect you in the long run rather than thinking about how they're going to make you feel right at this moment. Dinner will be in about ten minutes, Martin."

After she left him, Martin thought about what she had said and burst out laughing. She had just scolded him in a way that he was sure she didn't realize. Standing up, he decided he was going to find the children and hang out with the rest of the family. And as of the moment Yasmine left him, he thought he was a part of a wonderful family.

~*~

"I'm not sure what you want from me, Mr. Billows, but I'm not even in the state right now. I asked for and got approved to have this weekend off. I have to settle my brother's estate." Mr. Billows told her she had one hour before she was to report to work. "Not possible. As I have said to you numerous times now, I'm not going to be able to come in. For a great many reasons, but not being in the state should be enough to tell you I'm not going to make it."

"Gracie, I'm sick of dealing with your shit all the time. You had better be in here at the beginning of this shift, or you should start looking for another job. Employees like you are a dime a dozen." She let out a long breath. He couldn't just replace her, and she knew it. "What do you have to say to that?"

"What do you think?" He told her she was a smart girl for doing what he demanded. "No, you got it wrong. I'm not going to be coming in tonight or any other night. I'll be contacting the owner tomorrow as well. If you're really that short-staffed, Mr. Billows, you should wait tables yourself. I'm finished."

It felt good to hang up on the man in mid-sentence. Before she could allow her doubts to settle in with her, she called the owner. Since she knew he'd be home today, it didn't bother her to call him at home. He had given her the number.

"Mr. Anderson, my name is Gracie Jefferies. I work at your restaurant called Devonshire. Mr. Billows just made it, so I've had to quit the restaurant, and I wanted to give you my side before he painted me as a bad person. I might need a reference from you or something. I doubt he'll do anything but slander my name four ways from Sunday." Mr. Anderson laughed, and she had to smile. He laughed like he didn't care one bit. "Yes, well, on my side, it's not all that funny. I explained to him that I had to settle my brother's estate for the bloodsucking attorneys. I haven't any idea why it has to be settled right this minute. As far as I can see, he didn't have a pot to piss in, much less the fancy name they're calling the estate. And I had asked for and was approved for the next four days off. I should be getting paid for it, as I've never had a day off in over sixteen months. I had to work the day we buried my brother." Gracie realized she was babbling and told the man what had happened.

"Gracie, did he ever allow you to train him on the closing procedures of the place? Or, for that matter, how to make out a schedule? Work that he should have been doing and wasn't?"

"I couldn't even try and show him how to rotate stock in the big fridge. He said whatever came out of the storage place would be used before its date, and I was to just leave it alone." He asked her if she'd done that. "No. Of course not. I know better than that. But I did ask for the time off, sir. I have the approval slip he signed the day I turned it in."

"I have no doubt that you have. And please accept my condolences on your brother's passing. I didn't know." She said he'd been sick for a long time. "Still, it is tragic. Let me know what attorney's office you're working with, and I'll find out what all the rush is about. That way, you can focus on what you're there to do. Where are you, anyway?"

"Ohio. A little town that no one has heard much about called Trinway." He laughed again. Gracie was beginning to think the man was off his rocker or something. Finding everything funny wasn't sane. "Anyway, you don't have to do that. I'll go there and take care of whatever they need, then clean out his house. I have to put it on the market as well right away, as he had built up medical bills more than the fund he was drawing on could cover. I have no idea why I'm telling you this."

"It sounds to me like you needed to vent, and I was the perfect person to do it to. But I know Trinway, Gracie. It's not far from Dresden, where I'm currently living. With my wife and brothers. I can get things taken care of for you right now." Again, she told him he didn't have to do that. "I don't. But I think you've done me a large favor by quitting your job today and finding out what Mr. Billows can do without you there running things for him. He's going to be in deep shit when the doors open, I think. Can you stay at your brother's place? Or do you need accommodations? I can do that for you if you wish."

"No, I can stay at my — what the hell is wrong with you?" He laughed again, and she felt her temper fall over her mouth. "You've done nothing but be nice to me since you went to the restaurant that I worked at. Now you're being nice about my brother dying, getting me an attorney, and finding me digs to stay in. No one in their right mind is that nice."

"My wife would agree with you. But my mom

taught me to help those that needed a hand up. She made it her life's work to do that. As for helping you in particular, you've been very nice to me in calling me and telling me the restaurant might be closed down tonight. Because as much as I'd like for the man to fail, he'll take my place with him. But only for tonight." She asked him if he could afford that. "I can. Even if I couldn't, it's a better way of him getting terminated than me calling him and doing it on— Ah. There he is now. Calling, no doubt, to tell me what a horrid person you are and that I should be grateful he's fired you."

"He didn't fire me. I'm sure it would have come to that, but Mr. Billows gave me an ultimatum that I couldn't work with. So I quit."

He asked her to hold on if she could. Telling him she could, Gracie watched the people playing in their yards while she waited.

Charlie had been ill since he was a child. He had fallen out of a tree at the daycare center where the two of them had been taken while their parents worked. Charlie had been about four, not that she ever believed he'd been climbing a tree in the first place, but he had hit his head. Hard enough, her parents had been told that it cracked his skull. Since they'd had no insurance that would cover something like that kind of major surgery for a clumsy kid — they'd not even offered it to them — they'd not been able to afford for him to have whatever would be necessary for him to live.

To this day, she believed that one of the adults working at the daycare center had hurt him. The government not only provided her family with a food card, but they had paid for daycare so they'd not be a total burden on society. The insurance was all right — it covered a lot — but not nearly what they needed at that time.

Charlie could live alone only with someone coming in once a day to check on him. He could function well enough to work at a menial job, so long as it was repetitive and wasn't something that had to be done in a timeframe. He could do it; Charlie would work at a job all day and night, but once he was off the task for more than a few minutes, he'd have to be trained all over.

When Mr. Anderson came back on the phone, he asked her if he could message her something to her phone. Telling him that was fine, she wasn't sure what he'd have to say to her in a message that he couldn't say while they were speaking. Then he explained.

"That's the name of the attorney that is going to meet you at Bickerton and Bickerton in the morning. Arthur is a good attorney and a good friend. He said you were to dress casually, not dressed up. I'm not entirely sure why, but that's what he told me to tell you. Also, would you mind letting him make a copy of your permission slip from Billows? He's claiming you are fabricating all of this." She said she wasn't a liar. "I know that. All right. He's going to pick you up in the morning. I've already given him the address where you're staying."

"And just how did you come by that information?" His laughter again made her want to smack him. "Look, Mr. Anderson, I no longer work for you, so why the hell are you doing this? For a sense of enjoyment on my part? I won't think it's funny if I have to find my own way to the office in the morning and find out that being late or some shit is forfeiting whatever little bit my brother had to them. I think they're crooks, but I don't know a great deal about bloodsuckers."

"I have the best bloodsuckers in the world working for me. If I didn't, I'd not be as wealthy as I am." She told him to fuck off. "Thank you for that. It's refreshing to hear someone that isn't the least bit impressed by me or my money. I'll see you in the morning, Gracie. Good luck tomorrow."

After ringing off with him, she sat there long enough to look Mr. Anderson up. Whistling about what the news articles said about his money, she put her phone away. Not that she felt any better about him helping her, but she knew now that he could well afford it.

Starting her rental up, she made her way to her brother's home. When their parents had died, there had been a little money put away. They'd also been able to afford to purchase them a little house that just happened to be in a place that was developing into a nice neighborhood. She'd been able to sell it for about ten times more than her parents had paid for it and buy the house that Charlie was living in. Having it outfitted for his needs took all the rest of the money.

Going into the house, it occurred to her that this would be the last time she was here before selling it off. That her brother, her hero, wasn't going to come around the corner and tell her to wipe her feet. Wiping at her tears, she turned her phone off when Mr. Billows's name came up.

There wasn't much in the place that she'd have to deal with. Clothing, of course. His books too. Charlie loved to read when he needed to unwind. She did as well. The furniture had to be taken care of. Mostly she thought she'd give it away or donate it. Gracie thought someone could use it.

Getting her things out of the car, she pulled out the large trash bags she'd had at home and started in his bedroom. It took her nearly two hours to bag up items that still smelled like Charlie.

At about six, someone knocked on the door. While she wasn't sure if the neighbors knew her brother all that well, she went to check to see who was there. Opening the door, knowing that small towns weren't as safe as everyone assumed they were, she left the chain on the door.

"Ms. Jefferies, my name is Arthur Fowler. Mr. Anderson, Caleb, sent me here to bring you some dinner, and I'd like to go over any information you might be able to help me with concerning your brother's health and his estate." She opened the door wider and asked to see his identification. "Yes, of course. I should have thought of that."

After checking it out, she allowed him in the house. Before she could close the door behind him, he waved for the people she'd not seen to come into the house as well. They were delivery people. The smells coming from the many bags they had made her realize she had not just skipped breakfast but lunch too.

The food was spread out before them. As Arthur set his laptop to the side, he asked her about Charlie. Stuffing her face while answering him, she realized the man was a good attorney. He seemed to know his shit.

After telling him about the accident, as well as the names of the people that had worked there, she got up to find the file she'd left here with her brother, in the event she could ever get him an attorney.

"This will be very helpful. I have too that your parents had filed for a wrongful act, naming the daycare as negligent. Do you know if anything became of that?" She told him that they were turned away from every attorney they asked for help. "This isn't the way I do things, Ms. Jefferies. I get to the bottom of things regardless of what someone might want me to do."

"My parents did try." He told her he wasn't saying they hadn't but that the attorney should have done it regardless of if there was money or not. "Yeah, there isn't any of that either. I know Mr. Anderson said he'd pay you, but I'd like it if you were to send me the bill. I don't have a job right now, but I can work anywhere and do a good job."

"I'm sure you give every task all you can when assigned." Even after all the food was eaten and leftovers put away, they talked. It was nearly nine at night when Arthur stood up to leave. "You've given me more than I think I could have found in files for this. I'll be by in the morning to pick you up. I'm staying at Caleb's tonight, so I'll be close if you think of something."

"I don't know what else it would be. I think we've covered about anything and everything." She smiled when he laughed. "I'll see you in the morning."

After he left her, she found her old bedroom that she used when she came to stay with Charlie. There was very little in the room. An empty dresser.

A closet with hangers that looked like a row of flowers they were so colorful. Finding one of Charlie's large shirts, she pulled it over her head and laid down on the bed. Tomorrow was either going to break her or let her start over. She wasn't sure she'd get either, but it was a hope.

Gracie thought of her family. Her parents had tried so hard to make their lives better. They were making some headway into having money put away for a few things, like a vacation, when Charlie had been hurt. They'd not been able to take any vacations, of course, but they had always made time for their children.

In the summer months, they'd have picnics at the local parks. Go fishing at the dam. A great many free things that seemed like the world to them. A large basket of treats, Mom's jams, a ham sandwich or two, and a bottle of water was their meal when out like that.

Mom made quilts for their beds. Dad could repair anything and everything. That was where most of the extra money had come from was Dad knowing how to fix something. Everyone in the neighborhood knew to take it to Dad to be repaired, while Mom knew how to take something in and let it out when it came to clothing.

What they didn't have in material things, they certainly had more than enough love to go around. Twice that she could remember, they'd taken in a child or two. Just until their parents could find a job. Mom babysat too and helped with tutoring.

Everyone that came in contact with them respected them and liked them. They were the best. Now she was the only one left, and it made her sad to think that when she died, that would be the end of the Jefferies that she was related to.

Turning over on the bed, she looked out the window that was at eye level. Even for as late as it was, children were playing outside. She rarely saw a kid where she'd been working without a phone attached to their ear or looking down at it. The kids were catching firebugs. They weren't keeping them but catching and then releasing them. Gracie had done the same thing when she'd been little.

Remember to set her alarm so she'd get up in the morning, she turned her phone back on. Always surprised that it would come on, she set it for seven. Not bothering with the messages she had on it, she watched the children more. They were much more entertaining than anything that Billows had to say to her.

Charlie had been gone for a month now. The woman who came in to check on him had called her one morning, sobbing about how he'd fallen asleep and not woken. Even as she tried to calm the woman down, Gracie felt her heart shatter. It was the hardest call she'd ever taken.

In that month, she'd been working herself to death to be able to afford a ticket to come here to do this last thing for him. Affording the ticket to come here for his funeral had nearly bankrupted her. But she'd made do with eating her free meal at work and taking any leftovers home that the cook had saved for her.

Then Billows found out about the free meals. The next afternoon there was a sign put up that there would be no more freebies for anyone. She'd been the only one that qualified for the meal, as she was the only full-time waitress there. Not because she was scheduled to be full-time, but covering both Billows' and the day manager's schedules when they decided to just not show up was the only perk she got. He'd also taken her overtime away from her.

Gracie had almost stopped doing the job of three people when she realized that if the place shut down, which she was sure would happen, there would be a lot of people out of work. There were seven waitstaff as well as kitchen help, cooks, and the busboys that depended on the place having their doors open. She couldn't have done that to anyone.

Every week she'd get paid for thirty hours, what she'd been scheduled for, and all the other seventy plus hours would be free. Not that she didn't keep track of the hours she wasn't being paid for. She wrote every shift down, and even the extra time she had to do at home by making schedules, ordering food for the place, having carpets replaced when needed, repairs done, as well as a lot of other jobs the manager should have been taking care of.

Gracie had been working there for ten years. She knew the place better than the people who had built it, she'd bet. Gracie was upset about the things she'd been doing and how she'd been treated. Pulling her mom's quilt up to her nose, she inhaled deeply of the scent that was still there. Sunshine. It calmed her more than anything else.

It was nearing midnight when she felt she might be able to close her eyes for a few hours. She really hadn't slept well since she'd gotten the call about Charlie being gone. Crying herself to sleep, she let the tears fall while she willed herself to sleep.

AWARD WINNING, BESTSELLING AUTHOR

Kathi Barton, a winner of the Pinnacle Book Achievement Award and a best-selling author on Amazon and All Romance books, lives in Nashport, Ohio, with her husband, Paul. When not creating new worlds and romance, Kathi and her husband enjoy camping and going to auctions. She can also be seen at county fairs with her husband, who is an artist and potter.

Her muse, a cross between Jimmy Stewart and Hugh Jackman, brings her stories to life for her readers in a way that has them coming back time and again for more. Her favorite genre is paranormal romance, with a great deal of spice. You can visit Kathi on line and drop her an email if you'd like. She loves hearing from her fans. aaronskiss@gmail.com.

Follow Kathi on her blog: http://kathisbartonauthor. blogspot.com/